Beyond the Border

Edited by Farhana Shaikh

First published 2014 by Dahlia Publishing Ltd
6 Samphire Close Hamilton
Leicester LE5 1RW

ISBN 9780956696755

Selection copyright © Dahlia Publishing 2014
Copyright of each piece lies with individual authors © 2014

The moral right of the authors has been asserted.

All rights reserved. No part of this publication may be reproduced, stored in or introduced into a retrieval system, or transmitted, in any form, or by any means (electronic, mechanical, photocopying, recording or otherwise) without the prior written permission of the publisher. Any person who does any unauthorized act in relation to this publication may be liable to criminal prosecution and civil claims for damages.

A CIP catalogue record for this book is available from
The British Library.

Printed and bound by Grosvenor Group

This book is sold subject to the condition that it shall not, by way of trade or otherwise, be lent, re-sold, hired out, or otherwise circulated without the publisher's prior consent in any form of binding or cover other than that in which it is published and without a similar condition including this condition being imposed on the subsequent purchaser.

Beyond the Border

CONTENTS

Introduction	6
Thank You for Your Participation *Mahsuda Snaith*	9
What You see in the Mirror *Deepa Anappara*	20
Faulty Goods *Farhana Shaikh*	36
Follow Your Dreams *Farrah Yusuf*	47
X *Jocelyn Watson*	58
You, in the Fading Light *Amna Khokher*	74
The Owl *Reetinder Boparai*	86
Nine *Nilopar Uddin*	96
Runaway *Rosie Dastgir*	115
The Baby *Huma Qureshi*	127
Table for Two *Susmita Bhattacharya*	144
My Brother Vrinder *Palo Stickland*	151
Don't Tell the Children *Priya Khanchandani*	160
Author Biographies	*175*

Introduction

In 2012, The Asian Writer ran its first short story competition. There was no way of knowing at the time, the standard of writing we would receive. Soon after the deadline, I read through each of the entries, nervous and then later, delighted. Competitions are never easy things to judge, but I was confident that we had found some real gems; talented writers who would go on to write more, achieve wider audiences. I'm pleased to say, many of them have. I produced an anthology of the entries, and *Five Degrees* was launched at the South Asian Literature Festival that same year.

We ran the same competition again in 2013 but I have to admit the entries were mostly disappointing. I had for some time thought about working more closely with talented emerging writers, to challenge them to extend their creative pursuits, to exercise that writing muscle. What emerged was 'Project X' – an online writing programme hosted by me to do just that. Many of the writers previously published in *Five Degrees* were invited to take part.

Early on in the process, I encouraged writers to write morning pages. There was general discord – many of them hated the process and probably me at the time. Having discovered the morning pages a year before I had seen a complete transformation in my ability to sit down and write. I wanted to gift the experience to this writing group. Sitting down and writing was and still is my biggest challenge. I had abandoned the morning pages since and found that coming back to them was wonderful. The writers who did embrace them found them to be useful. We set ourselves short term and long term goals, listened to short stories, did writer ly things like exercises, brainstormed ideas and shared short pieces of fiction. We communicated rather unsuccessfully on Google Plus. Overcoming the technical phobias were just part of the challenge.

Part of this 'experiment' (because that's what it was) was to see what would happen if you move writers out of their comfort zone, if you specifically say 'we want to publish something new, experimental.' Project X was explicit in its intention. During the process there was a focus on trying something new, being different. Phrases like 'tackling new ground' and 'experimental' were used. It wasn't just about shifting the goal posts but about awakening our selves to new experiences – each week writers were encouraged to go on dates, as advocated by Julia Cameron in her book, *The Artist's Way*.

Beyond the Border is a result of months of working together, sharing and editing each others work, moving perhaps closer to some sort of truth in our writing and finding our voice. Unlearning the rules we're taught isn't always the easiest thing to do, but I hope you will see hints of an attempt at trying.

Each writer emerged from the process with their own view on what is considered to be different, what exactly is tackling new ground or experimental and this evident in the originality and diversity showcased in this anthology. As editor I was delighted with the results. I'm not sure if some would have been written at all had it not been for that early encouragement to try something new. Each writer has taken on a challenge and the finished stories are brave and unexpected. Many writers have chosen to play with structure, others - narrative and subject.

Included alongside the stories written during 'Project X' are stories by emerging writers, Rosie Dastgir, Susmita Bhattacharya, Jocelyn Watson and Huma Qureshi which were invited through an open call. For those interested in hearing from each individual writer you can read a reflection piece on The Asian Writer website. It's been an incredibly exciting anthology to put together. Enjoy!

Farhana Shaikh
Editor

Thank You for Your Participation

Mahsuda Snaith

Good morning and welcome to our survey. Please sit down. You'll find a glass and some water to your left. Comfortable? Good. Let's begin.

Just to let you know this survey is being conducted by Cronos Core Ltd. You haven't heard of us? I'm not surprised. We like to keep low-key. I'm Yasmin, you're facilitator today. If you have any queries please ask, I'm here to make this process as smooth as possible. Cronos Core highly values your opinions and, as indicated in the information material, will reward you adequately for your time. You chose the chocolates? Fabulous decision. Most people go for the holiday voucher. Yes it is rather limited. That's right, you pay towards the final amount. Very good of you to read the fine print. A lot of people don't do that.

Now let's not waste any time. We want you to know that here at Cronos Core your answers will be kept strictly confidential. We are completely independent from the Ministry. That's right, completely anonymous. We really have no interest in anything other than your opinions. Your opinions are very important to us.

How do we keep independent? I'm sorry, I don't know what you mean. Yes, the Ministry does see everything. It's their job to protect us after all. Let's just say Cronus Core is a *separate* organisation.

Have some water. Relax. Now I can see your knee jittering there but really, you mustn't be nervous. These are very straightforward questions.

Ready? Fantastic.

Question 1. How would you describe your home?
a) A pigsty
b) A little untidy
c) Mostly tidy
d) Immaculate

You say *B: a little untidy*. Yes, things can pile up sometimes but you try and keep on top of it do you? That's fantastic.

Question 2. When working in a group which role do you prefer?
a) Leader - I enjoy managing people.
b) Secretary - I prefer to do paperwork
c) Presenter - I love public speaking
d) No role - I avoid group work as much as possible

Please don't spend too much time thinking about the answers. The first thing that comes to mind is just fine. *B: Secretary.* That's what you currently do is it? At the Ministry? You mustn't say 'just' admin. Administration is vital to the whole governing of our society. I suppose you would call this administration wouldn't you? Me ticking these boxes. Seems meaningless but it keeps the machine ticking. Vital work, yes. Now let's have a look.

Question 3. When you daydream, which of these do you mostly think about?
    a) How things used to be
    b) How things could be
    c) How things should be

Do you want me to repeat the question? Really, like I said, the first thing that comes to mind. B you say? Are you sure about that? You look unsure. B it is! *How things should be.* What's that? Oh dear, you're right, b was how things *could* be. How silly of me. Are you sure you want to stick with that answer? It really is no problem if you- No, that's fine. We'll move on.

Question 4. When I see someone who is destitute e.g. homeless, I feel sorry for them:
    a) Strongly disagree
    b) Disagree
    c) Agree
    d) Strongly agree.

The first answer that comes to mind please. Well yes, I do suppose it depends on the situation but we only have these four options. Really I must insist you don't overthink it.

Alright, let's make it easier. Say you walk outside and there's a homeless person on the steps asking for change. Man or woman? Do you think that makes a difference? No, I didn't either but let's say woman. *C: Agree.* No, there isn't a right or wrong answer, just whatever you instinctively feel is right for you. Yes, go ahead and have some more water. I'm perfectly fine thank you.

Question 5. How true is the following statement? *'When solving a problem, emotions should be ignored.'*
  a) Strongly disagree
  b) Disagree
  c) Agree
  d) Strongly agree

I know I keep saying this, but you really *must not* overthink the answers. We are only interested in your immediate response. You don't make *any* decisions? Ha! There you go again with your 'just' admin. Yes, I'm sure you only ever follow direct instructions. Don't we all? But what about other decisions you make, like what to wear in the morning? How to deal with difficult work colleagues? Well, we all have difficult colleagues. You say you don't but you can't get along with everyone can you? It's not exactly *unbelievable* just highly improbable. We are driven by human nature of course, it makes us very irrational creatures. Yes, I'm sure you do try and be rational. But rationales vary from person to person and I'm sure there are times you've found your logic clashing with another person's logic? You can't think of any occasion? How very interesting. In any case, you say *C: Agree.* Are you absolutely sure? No, reason, it's just- No really, it doesn't matter.

Question 6. When presented with a set of rules to live by, do you generally:
    a) Follow the rules
    b) Only follow the rules if it makes others happy
    c) Ignore the rules
    d) Make your own rules

Oh my, that was quick! A very definite *A*! I know, I said I wanted your initial answer and that's exactly what you gave me isn't it? *Follow the rules*, that's what you say. Which is strange considering the incident…I really shouldn't say anything. Not my business of course. I think you know what incident. The one in your office? Earlier this week? Let's be more specific then: the one with the staple-gun. Ah, that's jogged your memory. Oh yes, I realise you reported it as an accident. Just a mistake. Human error as they like to say at the Ministry. You must always allow for human error! Strange though that it was your manager's hand you had the error with? How do I know? I was told of course. Yes, we are part of a separate company but we're given certain *information* before we carry out our surveys. You see, here at Cronus Core we're very interested in human behaviour. And your behaviour of course. You must have noticed you were the only one asked to participate in your department? I really couldn't comment on the reasoning. Let's just say there's a *selection process*.

Now, let's move on. Although I do wonder. No, it doesn't matter. Move on we shall! Except. It's just, I'm sorry, it's playing on my mind. I'm just wondering why you had the staple-gun in the first place. No, it's not a question on the survey. Just a niggle really. You see, I thought you needed to be authorised for certain office equipment and from the information we were given it's obvious you don't have the clearance for anything other than basic admin. That would mainly include photocopying and computer processing. In fact there is nothing in your remit that would necessitate the use of a staple gun. So again, I just wonder why you had it in the first place. I know your time is limited. That's true of all of us of course! Still, I'm sure if you explained it to me quickly…You'd prefer not to? Of course, that is your prerogative. Let's have a look here. Ah, yes.

Question 7. If you were working with a group of people, and you had to create a rule for how decisions would be made, which of these would you choose?

    a)   Decisions always made by group consensus

    b) Decisions always based on the undisputed facts
    c) Decisions always based on a majority vote
    d) Decisions always based on a senior members' decision

That is a hard one isn't it? I'll let you think about it seeing as it is your final answer. I suppose it's a bit of a philosophical question really. I suppose all of these are. How should people *behave*? That's what we're asking you here at Cronos Core. How, in your opinion, should people conduct themselves in our civilised society? Of course fitting in is very important. This modern day myth of the 'individual' is really quite ridiculous. One of the reasons we've evolved into the superior creatures we have is because our ancestors learnt to work in packs and when working in packs were assigned certain roles. Roles are very important of course. We've done a lot of research on the subject. Yes, I do have a point. I'm getting right to it in fact. Please do have another drink.

Like I was saying, roles are very important. Say you were a caveman and you wanted to catch a mammoth. You can't have one man running off with a spear can you? How much use is that against a gigantic mammoth? No. You need to work in a group, in a *team* so to speak. And in a team there is always a leader. You can't have all the hunters running the show can you? By the time you came to a decision the mammoth would have run off into the distance! It is more efficient to have roles, don't you find?

There is a hierarchy, and if you want the best results you need to know your place in it. And stick to it of course, you must stick to your role in the pack. Oh dear, I really have gone off topic. We're just so fascinated about this subject here at Cronus Core. The subject of human behaviour that is. But I must let you get on. You're a busy worker. A vital and very busy worker. Your answer then? Ah, yes I suppose you have forgotten the question. I'll summarise.

If you were working with a group of people and needed a rule for decisions would you choose: *Group consensus, undisputed facts, majority vote* or *a senior member's decision...*

None? You say none of those options. Well, I'm afraid 'none' is not an option. Why not? Because surveys don't work that way. We give you simple questions with multiple-choice answers and you must choose one of the answers provided or the system doesn't work. How else are we supposed to collect the data into any viable quantity? How are we to say 50% of people surveyed said they described their house as a pigsty if everyone said, well no actually mine is more like a bird's nest or a rabbit warren? There isn't any room for subtleties in surveys. There are stock answers and you have to choose what you feel describes you best. Now shall I ask that question again?

No? Then please, you're answer

Ah. You say none again. Now, we are both busy people here and I'm sure you'd like to get back to work. You wouldn't? You wouldn't like to get back to work. And why is that exactly? Well that is an interesting word to call you're manager. And you're colleagues too! A whole host of interesting words there. I thought you said you got on with your colleagues, no problems at all.

You lied? Can I just clarify that you're admitting to lying in this survey? This survey, I must point out, that is being carried out on behalf of the Ministry. Yes I did say it was independent. The Ministry does not run Cronus Core, they just commissioned the survey. That was explained in the information leaflet. In any case, here at Cronos Core we have an active interest in the concerns of our clients. Of course your answers are strictly confidential though if asked to give general comments we are usually compliant. Again those conditions were clearly stated in the information leaflet. It's very important you read the fine print don't you think? So, yes, we usually give a *report* back to our clients. Your name is kept strictly confidential of course, though the timing on the sheets will probably correlate with your agreed absence from work. What will be in the report? Well I can't really comment. Let's just say a brief outline of your opinions. Your opinions are very important of course. They greatly reflect the attitude of staff towards the Ministry and therefore are reflective of the Ministry itself. Which of course affects the running of the country when you think about it. And in these unsafe times the Ministry tries so hard to keep its citizens protected you could almost say these surveys are a matter of public safety. Administration is at the heart of the machine and we wouldn't want any parts of that machine to be faulty. If they were then those parts would need to be disposed of as quick as possible so as to prevent any serious damage. Disposed, yes, and replaced straight away. That just makes sense doesn't it?

Now can I ask that question again? You are willing to admit right here and now that you have lied in this survey? I'm afraid there's no more water. If you could please answer the question. I must insist you state your answer and not just shake your head. We wouldn't want any room for ambiguity would we?

Ah. You say you haven't lied? And you have an answer for the question? *D* you say? That would be *a decision based on senior member's decision.* Interesting, considering you were so unsure before. An error you say? You made an error. And the comment about your manager? And you're work colleagues? Errors too. That is rather a lot of errors for one question. It's true, you must always allow for human error. Especially with administration of course! As the Ministry states, human error is after all only *human*. But, as the Ministry also states, we must ensure they don't become a habit. We must make sure that we keep our errors to a minimum. Don't you agree? I'm glad you agree.

Yes yes, that was the final question. Well done! You have earned yourself a rather lovely box of chocolates which you can collect at the reception desk. Don't eat them all at once! Share them with your colleagues perhaps? Or give them as a little 'sorry' to your manager? Of course I know it was an accident, but still…I'm not *telling* you what to do. It's simply a suggestion. Yes, of course the chocolates are to do with as you wish. Now there's no need to get emotional, they're only chocolates. I know they're *your* chocolates. You earned them, yes. Here at Cronus Core- Now, please there's no need to raise your voice. It would be a shame for you to sabotage what has turned out to be a very successful survey. Well, maybe 'sabotage' is a little strong. There's no need- Can you please sit down? I must ask you to lower your voice. I am going to ask you one more time…What will I do? Let's not find out what I'll do. No, it's not a threat, it's a *warning*. If you could stay on your side of the desk please. Now, put that down. Put the jug-

Security! I need security! Get in here n-

What You See in the Mirror

Deepa Anappara

THE BOY—
—had been hoping for a mobile phone on his fourteenth birthday but what he got instead was a book that claimed to be 'Food for the Brain', a T-shirt with the word 'handsome' printed as black and stout as an elephant leg, and a small oval mirror housed in a wooden frame with two identical peacocks perched on top. It was an old mirror, perhaps as old as his grandfather, whose gift it was. He leaned the mirror against the window and squinted at his reflection. The tube light above him buzzed and blinked.

A mobile he could have used to impress his girlfriend. A mirror he would have to use to impress her with his ekdum hero-like looks. He dipped his fingers into a tumbler of water and spiked up his hair. Then he put on the sunglasses he had purchased from a roadside vendor and arranged his features to form a grimace in the manner of the brooding film stars he had seen on posters. He looked fine. Handsome even. His girlfriend would agree.

The Woman who once owned this mirror had also been someone's girlfriend. She was famous in these parts; more infamous than famous really. His grandfather had been the driver of the bus that the Woman – then only a girl – had taken to the city, running away from her home with three hundred stolen rupees in her purse and a bastard baby curled up in her belly. What a scandal. Even now when people talked about her, their faces crimped involuntarily, and their voices dropped, slow and smooth like kites gliding down with flared talons to snatch their prey. They called her a good-time girl who had somehow (*we know how, yes-yes, but we can't say it in front of our children*) got rich in the city and had come back after her father's death to sell off her ancestral home (*and what will she do with the money? Open another you-know-what in the city?*).

He could guess what they said when they thought he couldn't hear them. He was smarter than he let on. For instance, though his grandfather claimed he had paid a fortune for the mirror at a special sale the Woman was holding at her father's house, he knew he must have got it for almost nothing. His grandfather was a miser who opened his wallet only at the local theka.

Inspecting the shadow of a moustache above his lips, he wondered if the Woman had prettied herself in front of this mirror for the lover who had put a baby in her; the way he was dressing up now for his girlfriend, who must be waiting for him in the dark alley behind her house. The thought made him uneasy and he turned the mirror towards the window. Come on, he could do what he wanted, couldn't he? He was a boy. Unlike a girl, he had nothing to fear or lose.

THE GRANDFATHER—

—was not going to let anyone know that he had picked up his grandson's birthday present from a garbage heap. He sat on a charpai outside his son's house, wrapping a mirror in an old newspaper as his daughter-in-law hung out clothes to dry. He suspected the mirror was not a lavish enough gift to spare him her anger for a few days. When his son was not around, she grumbled about him living with them. He had had enough of it. But what could he do? His spine had crumbled from years of driving the night bus into the city. He barely managed to hobble to the bus stand to chat with the drivers alongside whom he had once worked.

A warm afternoon breeze ferried the smell of pulses and spices from a wood fire next door. He had just eaten lunch: two rotis with a tiny helping of carrot subzi, a meal so insubstantial his gut still felt hollow. Thank God for his friends at the bus stand. They bought him naan-khatai, suggested home remedies for his aches, and gave him their old mufflers and monkey caps. They had directed him to the sale at the Woman's house and, tottering over there earlier that afternoon, he had found the mirror in a trash heap next door. Maybe the Woman thought no one would want it and had thrown it away. A stroke of luck. Not like he had the money to buy a birthday present for his grandson.

He had been curious too, to be honest. In his mind, years of night-driving had meshed together into a vast swathe of black illuminated solely by the low beams spilling from the bus' headlights, but the night the Woman had taken his bus to the city? He remembered it in colour.

'What are you doing?' his daughter-in-law asked him now, holding an empty bucket in her hand, the sleeves of her red blouse stained dark by the water that must have dripped from the wet clothes.

'You know the Woman's back?' he said. 'I'll never forget the night she was in my bus. Cried so loudly everyone wanted to throw her out.'

His daughter-in-law frowned, looking as if she wanted to rebuke him for repeating a story that had already earned him several free pegs at the Desi Angrezi Daroo Theka near the bus stand. But she hesitated. Maybe she hoped he would have something new to add to his story this time, a warm morsel of gossip she could share with the neighbours.

'When we stopped for dinner, I went up to her and asked her what was wrong. If there was anything I could do to help,' he said. 'I was worried about her, you know.' The lies came to him easily. In his ears, they had acquired the roughness of truth.

In reality, after feasting on ghee-laden rotis and mutton curry at a dhaba that night, he had watched her sniffling from a distance. The bus conductor noticed him staring at her and said, 'Her lover boy, he had come to see her off at the bus stand. Looked like they were fighting. Must have promised to marry her and changed his mind.'

They lit their beedis, red tips flickering in the gloomy yellow light of street lamps, and tried to guess the reason for her tears. An unwanted pregnancy or a lovers' tiff? An argument with her parents or a new job in the city? Afterwards they had stubbed out their beedis and rounded up the passengers loitering around the dhaba. Throughout the journey, he had not spoken to the Woman even once.

'She didn't want anything,' now he told his daughter-in-law, who looked disappointed by the lack of drama. 'We realised what she'd been up to only days later. When the policeman came to the bus stand with her photo.' His daughter-in-law started to walk away, purposefully swinging the bucket in her hand, as if she wanted to whack someone with it. 'What a shock that must have been for her parents,' he added to her retreating back. 'Goes to show, no matter what you do for your children, you can never guess how they'll turn out.'

THE LOVER—
—took his wife and two sons to the Woman's sale because he wanted her to see he was 'settled'; in case she – somehow having turned up from somewhere – planned on looking him up. In the unkempt garden outside her house, amidst clumps of weeds, their feet tangled with sooty pots and pans and plates. Around them, cupboards, chairs and tables slouched on broken legs. His wife lifted up the edge of her sari with which she veiled her face and examined a frying pan.

He scanned the garden for the Woman but she wasn't there. Blood thumped in his ears. He thought of the evening he had seen her first, coming out of her sewing class at a government centre outside which he and his friends used to hang out. He had fallen in love with her that very evening, because she was beautiful, because she had held his gaze as if challenging him to look away, all the while sucking blood from what must have been a needle scratch on her forefinger. In two weeks she sneaked out at night to ride on his moped to an abandoned factory in the outskirts of their village, where they kissed under a tarry sky, ignoring the humming and biting of mosquitoes, and the snarling of a swarm of stray dogs tearing apart a chicken stolen from someone's coop. When they were leaving, the faint light of his moped picked up a line of bloodied feathers on the ground.

There were many nights like that one when her father was out drinking at a theka. He dreamt of a life with her, up until the night she told him her secret, so nauseating and gruesome he couldn't articulate it in his thoughts even after all these years. That night he had dropped her close to her home and told her never to bother him again. What else could he have done? They had been together for only seven months.

Now he saw her strolling out of her house with a small bag slung over her chest. She looked more stunning than she had when they had been teenagers. Her fair, translucent skin gleamed, and her brown eyes were framed by long eyelashes. She sported a modern, short haircut with a stylish fringe, and wore a dark-green salwar-kameez that clung to her curves each time the breeze returned towards her, drawn to her like a bee to a flower.

'Papa, can we buy this?' his eldest son asked, holding up a small, chipped wooden elephant whose ivory trunks seemed to have been sawed off.

'Put it back,' he said. 'It's useless.'

His wife was still holding the pan she seemed to fancy, caressing it as if it were a silk sari. She extended it towards him but he shook his head and started to walk towards the Woman. His sons and wife followed him. He picked up a mirror lying crooked on top of a mound of blankets and took out a twenty rupee note. From this close she smelled like oranges and lemons, just like the city girls who sometimes came to their village to take photos of farmers.

'I'll give you twenty rupees for this,' he said, thrusting his chest out to hide his nervousness.

'That's more than enough, thank you,' the Woman said, smiling in a distracted fashion, accepting the note without looking at him. She then turned towards an old man trudging towards her with a bed pan. 'Take it, take it,' she told the man. 'I don't want any money for it.'

Thank you?

That was all he got. As if they had never met before. As if he had not driven her on his moped to the bus stand on the night she had turned up outside the government centre, apologising for showing up, asking him if he could lend her a couple of hundred rupees. That night she had snapped at him when he told her running away was a bad idea. *You're a girl. Worse things will happen to you in the city*, he had said.

And it must have. He had heard the rumours about her like everyone else.

As soon as they walked out of the rusty iron gates of the Woman's house, he dumped her mirror in a trash heap. 'Termites,' he said. He wanted no sign of her in his home.

'We should return it,' his wife mumbled.

He felt sick. An iron fist seemed to be pounding his head.

His sons started to bicker about something. He was about to clout the back of their heads when his wife shushed them with the promise of kachoris laced with yoghurt for lunch. She was a good cook, his wife, his paunch a testament to the magic she worked in their kitchen. The Woman probably never cooked. Unlike his wife, she didn't have blisters or cuts on her hands. He had noticed it when she took the money from him.

His life was better without her, he was sure.

THE POLICEMAN—

—went to the Woman's house first thing in the morning because he didn't have anything better to do. He was disappointed to see how well she looked. In the years that had passed since he had last seen her, he had been promoted twice, but his hair and teeth had fallen out, his spectacle lenses had grown thicker, and his belly had become considerably rounder; so much so that shuffling forward was beginning to seem like strenuous exercise. Good thing no one expected him to chase burglars or anything (at least he was still holding onto his sense of humour).

The Woman was talking to someone when he entered the compound of the house, which was painted pink. Cracks slithered towards the ground along the walls. The smell of burnt plastic hung in the air. He wondered how the dead man's lawyer had managed to locate her. With computers, it must be. He didn't know how those things worked.

Though his khaki uniform made him conspicuous, he tried to avoid her by scrutinising an old radio, and thumbing through the time-stained pages of books with lurid covers. He picked up a mirror with peacocks in its frame and winked at his image. The citrus scent of a perfume wafted towards him, cutting through the bitter smell enfolding the garden. He turned around and saw the Woman standing next to him, eyes narrowed, lips tightened in a thin line.

'How are you?' he asked.

'Please leave,' she said, without raising her voice.

'I'm thinking of buying this mirror,' he said, holding it towards her.

'No,' she said and, snatching it from his hands, flung it on a sagging mattress piled high with tattered blankets.

Look at her gall. Not even his teenage sons dared to speak to him like that.

'You might have a fancy haircut now but you're still the same old slut you used to be,' he hissed at her, splattering saliva on her face. Good. She deserved it.

She stepped back, clenching her jaw. Others rooting through the things strewn around the garden, more interested in observing the Woman than the objects on sale, were watching them, mouths agape. She raised her arm and wiped her face against the sleeve of her kameez.

'Get out,' she said in English. 'Don't make me speak to your boss.'

A decade in the city seemed to have made an English mem out of her. He nodded at the others, as if to show he was still in control and, running a disinterested finger over the back of a chair, ambled out in a leisurely fashion. That would show her.

Outside the gate of the house, he stopped a motorbike that was carrying three men and a child. 'Where are you going? To shamshan ghat?' he sneered at them. They trembled in his presence, stuttered when they tried to answer his questions, and swallowed whole words altogether. It made him feel good. Not just good, but excellent. He let them off with a warning.

Walking back to the police station, he thought of the years of service he had put in, which the Woman had tried to undo with her callous words. All because of one afternoon years ago, when delirious, she had turned up at the police station with a malicious complaint against her father. He knew her type. Bunking classes to consort with boys. Making up God knew what atrocious stories so she could get out of housework and her studies. He knew her father; a good man if ever there was one. Still, he did his duty: interviewed her mother and brother, who contested everything in the Woman's complaint. They called her a liar; wicked to the core; twisted in the head. And that had been the end of the case as far as he was concerned.

At the police station, he sat down on his chair, feeling dizzy. The Woman was a witch; she must have cursed him. Soon after she left, a series of misfortunes had struck her family. Her mother died of what doctors initially thought was a minor stomach illness. Her brother sold off their farmland and cattle without telling the father and disappeared with the money. In his old age, the father had no one to look after him. He had died smelling of urine and shit, maggots eating his skin.

Something like that would never happen to him. He had a wife, a mistress, two sons, one daughter, and an extended family who, annoyingly enough, visited often to eat lunch or dinner with him. Still tonight he would sprinkle himself with Gangajal and go to the temple to make sure God had no reason to be unhappy with him.

THE WOMAN—
—threw open the windows of her parents' bedroom so the sun could reach parts that never seemed to have known light. The early morning sky was a sickly whitish-blue and the air smelled like cow dung and diesel. She could hear the rumble of tractors in the distance and, closer to the house, bells ringing around the necks of goats and cows heading out to graze under the usually indifferent gaze of their shepherds. A sound so familiar she wanted to claw her ears out. How was she supposed to live here until this house was

sold?

But she had to; she needed the money. Only the promise of a sum large enough to put down a deposit for her own flat in the city – a studio or a one-bedroom, nothing big – had brought her back to the village. Everything seemed unreal, this day unfolding in front of her, the phone call she had received three weeks ago informing her of her father's cremation, the bus journey back to this village that she had never expected to see again. Strange that the beast of a man she called Father had, well before his death, hired a lawyer in the nearest town. Stranger still that the lawyer had managed to locate her through the internet. When he called her up at the call centre where she worked in the city, the lawyer's lackey had said, 'You didn't disappear after all. You haven't even changed your name. How come the police never found you?' And before she could answer, 'I'm making friendship with you on Facebook, okay?'

This was her father's last gesture: leaving the house to her in his will just so it wouldn't go to his thieving son. A gesture of revenge, not apology.

Now every room in the house seemed darker and smellier than she remembered it. No amount of Lysol could cut a white arc through this dankness. In his dying years, her father had hired a maid to clean the house, she had learnt, but as his world became confined to his bed, the maid seemed to have ignored the tufts of cobwebs hanging from the ceiling, and the layer of dust coating the floor alongside the droppings of cockroaches and rats, and corpses of flies.

Someone was knocking on the front door. When she opened it, two men she had hired to move the furniture from the house into the garden were standing outside.

'You're early,' she said.

'We have to be if you want it done on time,' said the man who looked the older of the two, with wiry white hair and skin burnt black by the sun.

Their enthusiasm, she suspected, came from a desire to nose around. Not that they were going to find anything. 'Start anywhere,' she told them. 'I want everything outside. Except for the two suitcases you see in the hall.'

She picked up her handbag and slung it over her shoulder for safekeeping. 'Remove the stuff in the kitchen too,' she told them. For a small fee, a neighbour had offered to feed her until she could sell the house, which she hoped would be soon. Her boss had been reluctant to sanction even the two-week leave she had asked for.

The men grunted and swore as they carried a wide metal almirah through a narrow door. She busied herself by tearing down the grimy photographs of gods and goddesses her mother had glued to the walls, methodically moving from room to room, all her energy focused on her fingertips. She had always found it calming to repeat a gesture until she could perform it on autopilot.

Half an hour later, she found herself back in her parents' bedroom, facing a mirror with two peacocks carved on its frame, their heads turned away such that they would never have to look at each other. Her reflection startled her. Staring back at her from the mirror was the face of the girl she used to be. At once, her mind started to replay the scenes from her earlier life, their sudden intensity blinding her, throttling her, until she was down on her knees, biting down on her dupatta to stop herself from screaming.

Eleven. That was how old she had been when her father started. A pat on the head that swiftly turned into something else. His shadow looming on the wall at night as she sat turning the pages of a textbook. His pungent, loud breath in her ears as she kept her eyes wide open and focused on the gods on the wall. *Please please please*, she had prayed. *Don't let this be happening to me.* The gods didn't hear her. Nobody did.

For so many years she had believed it was her fault. Those around her had encouraged her to believe it. On some nights when she couldn't sleep, she would imagine confronting them: her mother who slapped her when she begged her to stop Father, her brother who threatened to break her arm for crying, a leering policeman who asked how much she charged for one night and, by the way, could he have a go too, and a boy whose lust and affection turned into revulsion the moment she told him what she was subjected to at home.

Enough, she told herself. Enough of despair. *Count backwards from twenty to zero. Think of how far you've come.* All those years ago, she had set out on her own to a strange city, knowing nothing and no one, found a place in a women's hostel, convinced the owner of a burger joint to hire her, and practised her English on young customers until she cleared a walk-in interview at a call centre. *You'll be a team manager soon. Who could have imagined that?*

One of these days she would look into the mirror and see the person she had become. One of these days she might even find love. She exhaled, wishing there was something she could do to make herself feel better *right now*. If only she could burn down this cursed house — but what good would that do?

She picked up a blue plastic bag lying on the ground, bundled some of her father's stinking-of-vomit-and-piss clothes into it and, holding it away from her body, carried it into the backyard. In three trips, she carted out most of his clothes. From the kitchen, she brought out a bottle of kerosene and poured it over the clothes and, with a gas lighter, set them on fire. The stench of burnt plastic mixed with that of fabrics. The harsh smoke made her throat itch.

'Are you okay?' she heard one of the men shout and turned around to see them staring out of a window, their faces pressed against the grille.

'Everything's fine,' she yelled back, though the smoke muffled her voice.

Something crashed to the floor as the men resumed their work. She watched the crackling flames reach for her as a gust of wind passed, and wondered why she didn't feel free or relieved. She wished for closure – *now that he was dead* – but perhaps it would come tomorrow or two years later or never. She had to learn to live with that.

Faulty Goods

Farhana Shaikh

Is there a difference between man and machine?
One is supposed to *think,* the other isn't *capable.*
Or that's what they taught us in a philosophy class I took last summer.

When I married you, you said so little that I begged you for conversation. Later I realised that you weren't programmed that way. Mum said you were just a bit on the quiet side and I should give it time. She said you would come out of your shell, as if you were a tortoise under threat. You seemed distant, aloof, mechanical even. I waited for a flicker of emotion, a twinkle, but accepted defeat when none came. You failed to load, stuck on a different level, leaving me second guessing.
'Men don't talk much, don't push his buttons,' warns Mum. 'Your persistence,' she reminds me, 'will come to nothing.'

Headstrong girl.
Stupid girl.
And then she throws me that disapproving look.

Pulling faces at grandma.
Smoking behind the bike sheds.
Flunking my GCSE's.
Found a husband online.

We met virtually. It's where we fell in love. Do you remember those days, and even longer nights we spent chatting, sending each other direct messages under the guise of our internet ids?
Me: Foxylady112
You: iRobot82

I remember that awkward conversation that started it all. I asked you why you put the year of your birth for all to see, and you replied, 'What's it got to do with you?' It was blunt like the knife I used to cut myself with, a bitter lemon that takes you by surprise. You were right. It had nothing to do with me.

Mum always said I was too nosy for my own good, that one day it would get me into trouble. But by then I'd learnt the art of humour and misdirection. I simply distracted you by asking another question, and then another, like an illusionist conjuring up his latest trick.

When you spoke it was only to answer my questions, never to think up your own. I should have known then that I would be the one to start the conversation; ask the questions. I didn't mind taking charge. You followed my lead. Understood me. Showed you cared. And unlike other men didn't play games. You gave me hope: always returned my calls. Your texts appeared in my phone, each one declaring your love for me; slowly hooking me in.

We connected. Clicked. Sparks flew. You captured something I didn't know existed. Stirred up feelings I didn't realise I had. Set me free. Made me feel alive.

You were strong, dependable, attentive.

We spent hours talking about the big things; politics, religion, the stuff that mattered, and the stuff that didn't. We killed time satisfying our curiosity, peeling back layers to reveal our core, surprising ourselves to see just how much we had in common.

Now, fingers on keyboard, eyes glued to the screen you rarely turn to look at me, mumbling inaudible whispers. You've become economical with words like I am with water, refusing to let it waste, saving it up in jugs. Yes or No are your most popular replies, followed by Nothing. And OK for everything else.

'How are you?'
'OK.'
'Is anything the matter?'
'Nothing.'
'Are you okay?'
'Yes.'
'Do you want anything to eat?'
'No.'

The empty silence hangs in the air widening the ever-growing gap between us.

'I'm surprised he can get a word in,' Mum says, 'with your blabber mouth. Men are either great listeners or great talkers. You should be so lucky.'

I cling on to those emails we sent back and forth, in our coffee-fuelled, insomniac ridden, misspent youth. Letters, longer than my arm in 12 pt Times New Roman, over-laden with emotions and dreams of the man you wanted to be. You wanted to write. You wanted to change the world.

And you did.

Your letters changed my world. Your ambitions were infectious, and you said everything with so much conviction that I didn't ever question you. I was too in love to do that. I didn't second guess myself, I simply fell in. I hold on to those missives now, mourning a life that's already passed, instead of toasting a future that's yet to begin.

'He's certainly different.' My friends said. 'Where on earth did you find him?' I laughed them off, dismissing them jealous. 'Be careful, he could be anybody,' they warned. I shunned their doubts pushing them aside.

The differences didn't seem to matter then. They only brought out the best in us, bound us together. But under this roof, it's the differences that have pulled us apart.

We've become complacent, disjointed.

I watch as you sit and stare at the television, hands glued to the control, wondering where things went wrong. We're malfunctioning, you and I. No longer in sync. Somewhere along the road our wires have crossed. Our fate forever skewed. You've lost that passion. The energy. The animation. The magic's disappeared.

You've lost the art of being human; unlearning the things you've been taught. No longer able to read my emotions; moving around in auto-mode.

I fear you don't know me at all.

I memorise your movements, the blueprint of your existence. You're running on a schedule that never changes. Never stops. You're stuck in a routine of military precision; on time, and by the book.

It's robotic. It's automatic.
Input. Output.
It is what it is.
It is what it has always been.
Me and You.
You and I.
The irony is something's changed.

I've only mentioned it a couple of times, because I don't want to face the ugly reality but have you lost interest in me, is that it? Have I become another commodity, redundant technology, something to be switched on and switched off at your convenience?

You laugh me off but do nothing to put my suspicions to bed, and when I press you further you accuse me of being a nag; of sounding just like my mother; say it's time for an upgrade.

I'm not something that can be easily replaced, switched off, thrown away, flogged for 99p on Ebay.

You hurt me.
Make me cry.
Walk away.

You look at me as if I've lost my sense of humour, but if that's your attempt at being funny, you've lost your touch. Your jokes sting me like mites – quiet, painful, invisible. It's a pain you'll never understand, never feel.

'Things change.' Mum says over the phone. 'Do you think your dad's the man he used to be?' I try and get a word in, but she's not having any of it. 'Don't ruin this too,' she says, reminding me of men that have come and gone. 'This might be your only chance. You can't have everything you want. You'll never find the *perfect* man.'

'Yes!' I shout down the phone adding, 'something's not right' long after the dead tone plays in my ear. It's too late. I'm standing in the kitchen, eyes burning as I stir onions, every bone telling me that things are not supposed to be like this. I silence that inner cry. A pan of boiling water reduces to a simmer.

We plod along. You and I. We move around each other as if one of us is a bomb that's about to explode. I pretend I'm okay. You pretend it's not a problem.

You're great around the house with chores: thorough and efficient. You excel in fixing things that are ready to be thrown out. Always cleaning, putting things back neatly where they belong. My books and your DVD's sit quietly on their shelves, ordered from A to Z.

But your behaviour grows ever more erratic. It's as though you're two different people, running on two different programs.

Program A. Program B.
At the flick of a switch you're somebody else.
A: the man I married.
B: the man I wish I hadn't.
Here and There.
Jekyll and Hyde.

I don't know why you keep apologising. Sorry for this. Sorry for that. Sorry for things that you did and didn't do. You sound like a broken record. It's become your answer for everything. I just asked you how you are – hello?

I avoid your gaze, afraid to read your expression, afraid to hear what you're thinking. You stare into your phone, a lost soul, scrolling the news, searching for answers you'll never find. Your puffy eyes tell me all I need to know, another late night in front of a screen: Xbox, TV, computer, anything but.

'Why don't you treat yourselves to a meal?' Mum suggests.

On a night out, our eyes rarely meet, as we sit glued to our seven inch screens, preferring the blanket of silence over intimacy. Bed slippers over high heels. Like an old married couple that can't bear to share, can't bear to touch.

'You're addicted.' I blurt out. My choice of words clumsy, but it's your lack of response that spurs my anger. 'It's an addiction and it's got to stop. It's me or the screen.'

Sometimes I think I made you up. The romance - a figment of my imagination. A virtual fantasy. Something I let myself believe.

'Don't you have a soul?' I shout. My anger climbs higher and higher, burning my tongue, my knees jerk. 'What kind of man are you?'

Maybe it's time to accept that we're just too different you and I?

We don't fit.

Love isn't enough.

Never is.

Never was.

We were doomed to fail. I set the bar too high, like stars in a moonlit sky, my expectations higher still. But I can't bear to lose you. I wish I could press the reset button, put things right, make them how they used to be.

'Don't settle for less,' my friends say. 'He's a shit and doesn't deserve you.' As kind as their words are, I discard them like I do rotten apples, tossed on to the compost heap.

If I could change things between us, I would.

If I could undo what is done, I would.

After the outburst, our home is like a reading room, the air sweet, a collection of hope and thought. Distraction works well. I pour my sorrows into reading a self help guide, hugging my knees, my mind busy with the How tos of Life and Love. You click away at the screen. Your eyes glazed over, your lights switched off in the fog.
What I 'need' is a paradigm shift apparently.
A change of perspective.

Be positive.
Be mindful.
Be grateful.

Input. Output.

These are my mantras, the things I focus on as I cling on to the fraying edges of us, putting the past in the past, doing my best to forgive and forget.

Troubleshooting offers temporary relief. We grow like stems; making room for the other until we fit. The ebb and flow of us returns.

In bed, our bodies do the talking. In the dark, eyes closed, every bit of you is real. We un-wrap parts of ourselves that we didn't know existed. Everything that has come before rendered meaningless.

Every word, spoken and unspoken.
Every action, made and unmade.

In the morning light, everything becomes clear.
The shadows that chase our denial have no place to hide.
We don't have to pretend any more or make up another lie.

The end when it comes is always sad.
Filled with regret.
If onlys and maybes.
I know it might sound cruel but I'm relieved.
Now I'm letting go, you're full of questions, incriminations.
Wanting to know this and that.
Whose fault is it?
Does it matter?
They're just questions.
Answers we'll never know.
The truth is we just aren't working, you and I.
We're finished.
It's over.
This is goodbye.

I'm grateful you held on to my secret, as if it were a jewel passed from one generation to the next. We smiled as we told everyone what they wanted to hear: we met on Shaadi.com.

I was desperate.

The only daughter unmarried at 30!
Past her prime!
Won't have babies now!

I bought a present to myself on my birthday. Paid for it online. Next day delivery. I tracked the parcel from the moment it left the warehouse until it landed on my doorstep. On the weekend I took out a screwdriver and built you, like a couple do a bookcase from Ikea. You were custom made, a popular choice on AutoHusbands.com; built to behave just like the real thing.

Mum found out. I knew she would. She was amazed and disgusted in equal measure. She helps put you back in the box, piece by piece, metal to metal, wires to wires. She smiles as I fill out the returns form putting a cross next to faulty goods. I kiss you on the forehead, tuck you in with the manual I never cared to read. Mum covers up the labels with sticky tape so the neighbours don't see. I've arranged a collection, asked for a refund. It was fun while it lasted, but we were never meant to be.

Follow Your Dreams

Farrah Yusuf

Welcome.
Welcome to a taste of my world.
If you have found this, the last of my lovingly placed and as you can see beautifully bound journals, you are very familiar with my work and have no doubt already given me a name. I hope it is not something crass like butcher or strangler. You'll have to forgive me as I no longer follow the news to know. I find it can be too distracting. Especially after all the inaccuracies in the media's coverage of my launch - so many exquisite details missed. Such a shame.
In case you are interested, which something tells me you are, I prefer the name Dream Catcher. DC for short. I have always enjoyed acronyms and initials, they lend themselves to the idea of selection well - for they are only understood by those in the know. As you must already know selection is something I care for. While we are on the subject of preferences, I like my work to be thought of as art. I will come back to this later, but for now it is important that you see that it is art. If you don't, you will always miss the majesty of the full image – which would be a real shame given how far you have travelled to find me.
As you can already tell this journal is very unlike the others.

There are no body part inventories or lists of the co-ordinates of all the places I monitored my sacrifices before I took hold. Well done on working that out by the way and finding your way to this - my gift to you. I am assuming you have by now understood how much work went into selecting each sacrifice. Yes, sacrifice. I like that word it has a wonderful raspy quality to it. Say it aloud. Go on. You know you want to. Let me make it easy for you. Sacrifice. Sacrifice. Sacrifice. There - you hear it don't you? That quality. Beautiful, isn't it?

Forgive me, I have made you work rather hard - what with all the different sacrifice types and locations. Now, I believe it is only fair I level the playing field somewhat. I intend to give you some clues and you will no doubt follow them. If you spot all the clues and follow them correctly you will win a prize. Now, now, you will have to wait to find out what the prize is. Patience is very important. Patience is a quality I have been generously gifted with. One of many gifts - I am sure you agree.

I believe it is only now fair to give you some background. For I believe in rewarding hard work. No doubt you have filled countless hours, evenings, weekends missing family celebrations and the like searching for my background so here it is. Generosity is often undervalued but I suspect you will not underestimate the value of what I am about to tell you. Play close attention and remember what I said about clues. This is much like telling you a story I suppose. Sadly one gift not bestowed on me is that of storytelling. I never had much time for it. Even as child. But I shall try my best. Be kind with your criticism for when we criticise we often miss what is right in front of us.

So we begin... I have not always had the urge to create art. It began with a dream. A simple dream that came to me for the first time a few days after I left university. Left what felt like a constant fog of monotonous conversations with peers who clearly thought noise equated to power. Myself, I prefer silence. I assume you know that. Sometimes I like to pepper it with music. Rarely with voices. I suppose the dream came to me because I was finally ready. Free from the shackles of my family and enforced socialisation. One of my other gifts had set me free. Mathematics. My rare abilities in that field led me to acquire the kind of wealth that gave me the freedom to ultimately focus on my art. Mathematics unlike other subjects lends itself well to a preference for silence. No discussions need to take place. A calculation is either correct or it is wrong. It either works or it doesn't. A few simple numbers, arranged well, can produce something profound. I digress, back to the dream. I ignored it initially. Preferring to focus my attention on my job. Back then the urge was like a soft murmur in the back of my mind. When I made my first real mathematical breakthrough the dream began to reappear from time to time. It was not long after I bought the kind of house you see in magazines (now, surely you don't expect more detail than that – I'm being generous but do not be greedy) that the dream grew in intensity. The urge grew in parallel. Developing into a dull but constant hum.

The dream was the same each time. Except that each time a new detail was added. Another pattern. Another calculation to be explored, to be expressed, to be enjoyed but overall to be admired. With each detail the image grew more vivid. As the image grew it fed the urge. Everywhere I went I heard people say to each other that you must follow your dreams so I heeded their advice. Here I am following mine. The wondrous nature of my dream is that you and the world are now following it too. Thus far I have shown you a mere fragment but the rest is coming, it is. It will most definitely be worth the wait. Trust me.

Before long the dream played through my mind even during the day while I faced a computer screen or during conference calls. No self-prescribed chemicals or herbs helped. Sweat would gather over my eyebrows as the dream unfolded and as it culminated I could feel a smile crawl through my lips until it rose to my cheeks. As the days went on the sweat ceased and the smile took over until finally I found my heart lifting and a feeling of calm envelop me. It was a deep sense of calm that elevated me, for the first time, from being functional to being present.

Eventually the dream stopped and my imagination took over fuelling the urge. My imagination as I am sure you have admired already is another of my many gifts. I began by making copious calculations, moved on to notes and translated those into drawings, before graduating to paintings in an attempt to capture every detail of the vision unfolded in my mind. Soon, the paintings did not satisfy the urge enough to give me that sense of calm I had started to crave. So I started making lists. The first item was to acquire my knives collection. I prefer to refer to them as my beauties. For that's what they are. I have left you one of my beauties at each sacrifice site so I'm sure you'll agree that the name fits. I expect you had to put them in those awful clear sandwich type bags. A shame really for they each glow when viewed in the sun. The blade of each one glistens in a different way. Try it. See for yourself. I had no idea how to begin such a collection so what does an intellectual do? Visit museums of course. I visited many. Lingered over exhibits. Observing and absorbing the carving preferences of medieval England and ancient China by way of Egypt, Russia and Mexico and many others of course. Glass cabinets sadly separated me from many beauties I would have loved to include in my own collection but, alas, my mother instilled such a deep sense of morality in me that try as I might I could not force myself to steal any. Instead, I drove, sailed and flew in search of beauties like those in my dream. The spear point blade with a partially serrated cutting edge and green marbled handle that I left beside the green eyed chubby blonde secretary, was my first acquisition. The green of the handle and that of her eyes matched exactly didn't it? I set it off against the blue cashmere sweater I dressed her in. I hope you noticed. If you didn't I must say I would be disappointed. It was unfortunate that I had to take one of her eyes but you'll see in time why that was necessary. It is a crucial piece of my final image.

My apologies, I have jumped ahead. I told you I am not very good at story telling. Let me retrace my steps. Where was I? Of course, the list. Once I had my collection of beauties I needed to give them a good home so next on the list was just that. I spent an age creating the shelves. They needed to be just so. Row upon row of beauties hung on steel hooks against an exposed brick wall. Pay close attention and soon I may invite you to see them. They are, I assure you, spectacular.

I must use this opportunity to make a confession. We have passed each other a few times you and I. Ah, now – wait, wait… before you delve into the recesses of your memory and try to retrace your steps let me assist you a touch further. Else you will struggle.

You first caught my attention in the crowd that gathered by the swings where I had left a beauty I was particularly fond of. And I must also confess a sacrifice I am not that proud of, my carving skills had yet to reach their peak. Do not get carried away with that little nugget. You will waste your time and mine if you do. Let me be clear, I do not make a habit of watching the public respond to my work. Well, my work in progress that is - for much more has yet to be done. The final unveiling is an altogether different matter but we will come back to that later. Where was I? Yes, my beauty. You will have admired it. Surely. You must have. Think back. Yes, that is the one. The knuckle knife with the brass handle and double edged blade. A World War II piece. You will know that already of course as you later traced its previous owner. I know you debated the manner and significance of that incident for some time. It was not a sacrifice, I assure you. It was merely an argumentative barrier of sorts that needed to be silenced. A hiccup. There have been a few hiccups but of course hiccups, by their very nature, come in a series. That beauty was an early acquisition but still one my mind cannot help but linger over from time to time. Alas the beauties collection is only amassed to be shared so I have learned, with the passage of time, not to get too attached. At the time however I parted with it reluctantly. You will have seen it matched the colour of the child's hair so well that I eventually saw that the two must be paired. It was only right. It was that hair, specifically the high frequency curl pattern - what I believe you will call ringlets - that needed to be acquired. Such perfectly formed tight curl revolutions. Mathematics at its best. As expected, not one fell out of place on all the days that I monitored her. I do hope you found my note on the mathematical patterns of hair structure educational – along with the removed body part inventory of course. I had initially planned on leaving my note by the swings but thought better of it. When I saw you for the first time later I knew why I had hesitated. It is important to trust one's inner voice. I like to think you learned something when I later placed it where only you would find it. Does it make you look at your mother's hair differently? Yes, yes it has hasn't it? How could it not. Nature loves mathematical patterns yet somehow people do not marvel in the way they should but they will. They will. Soon. You, you will help lead the way. To where? To me. To my work... my art. Of course.

Again I have jumped ahead, I can't seem to help it. Back to the swings, the presentation of that sacrifice was not my best work. On reflection, I could have carved the co-ordinate numbers much more neatly into her chest. The elasticity and frankly the softness of her skin was the problem. An unexpected complication - from which I have learned a great deal but a complication nonetheless. Adult skin is much more suited to my work but from time to time that of children does have some uses.

Yet again, I digress. Let me return to, us. It was the look on your face. I was compelled to select you. You were transfixed. It was a look shared by no one else till then. Till you. Now, do not waste time trying to work out if you saw me that day. You didn't. You wouldn't. One benefit of looking what people often call ordinary is that I can melt into backgrounds beautifully. The next time we met our forearms touched. Just for a moment. It felt, well electric. You were with your family shopping for Christmas presents. A tiresome business to say the least. Your oldest son was screaming loudly at the sight of a giant gingerbread house - you didn't even notice me. Pity. I would have expected that by age six he had grown out of that. You must invest some time in training him. Unfortunately I suspect your preoccupation with me has not assisted that much needed endeavour. The last time, you were drunk. Celebrating my capture. Pre-emptive, as it turned out. We sat just feet away from each other. Ironic don't you think? Don't get angry, your nostrils flare when you do. An unattractive trait.

Back to my initial work, it was, even I must admit somewhat clumsy – some, not all. Well by my standards. I do regret that my first few sacrifices made such a mess. On reflection, I believe it was due to a mixture of excitement and awe on my part. Unavoidable in many ways but as they say practice does make perfect. With perseverance I have now acquired skills any surgeon would be proud of. Not without discipline – another most fortunate gift. I have observed many people falter in making their dreams a reality by simply not applying enough discipline.

My last sacrifice seems to have derailed you somewhat. I don't really understand why given I that I was generous with my clues. I understand you were fond of her but emotions have their place. And our journey is not their place. Let me explain, a trident whilst not a traditional knife was a necessary exception to the rule as it was a most crucial piece in my collection. The missing piece in fact. Such trouble to locate an original and then deal with all the licences, shipping and security issues. Tedium. Look into it if you will. Use those connections you have so painstakingly built. I do believe it was worth it in the end, do you agree? You must. No? Perhaps with time. I assure you that sacrifice will have a key place in the final work. An honour. The next sacrifice will be a touch easier to find given the time we lost on the last.

As we journey forth I would urge you, and of course the others you will I have no doubt share this with, to remember that mathematics governs nature, patterns and crucially your perceptions of beauty. Mathematics is art. Art that is all around you. Don't let anyone tell you otherwise.

Alas here it is that we must part. Until next time - when we shall meet through numbers alone. If you arrange them well you will see something profound and be welcomed to the next level. It takes a special eye to see, quite literally in this case.

There is a café near here – overlooking the docks. As well as a spectacular view, it serves deliciously plump and juicy burgers that you must try. Enjoyed best at dusk. Venture and see. Time well spent. I suspect something shiny may catch your eye.

Look closely and there is plenty here for you to explore. With these few pages I intended to look backwards to go forwards and give you a flavour of what is to come. Now this journal is yours to fill as you wish. I like to think of it as us sharing the journey together. Bound by the same pages.

Don't bother looking for prints. As always, I was very careful. The hand writing is of my next sacrifice. She is the best yet. In her I found a piece of the calculation I have long been searching for. You will see.

As I said, the rest of the journal is yours to fill. Onwards together.

You're welcome.

Yours in anticipation.
DC

X

Jocelyn Watson

X and I were like twins though we weren't. We both have Mum's eyes: big, gentle and black, and her thick wavy hair; mine's longer than X's, though he always wished he could grow his as long as mine. We both have a tiny dark mole on our left cheeks. X hated it when I called it his beauty spot. He's actually a year younger than I am though you'd never think that to see us. I don't know why I said that because you will never see us together. X might as well be my twin because since his death I'm only half alive. I'm lost without him and I doubt I'll ever feel whole again.

Our folks grew up in Bombay, went to school in Bombay, attended the same church and ended up together at St Xavier's College. It came as no surprise to my respective grandparents when Dad, very old school, asked my grandparents if he could marry Mum. It was only when they agreed that he asked Mum. You just can't imagine that sort of thing nowadays. What followed was sort of anticipated. Dad got offered a job with IBM in London and Mum a teaching job with Smiling Computers. So amid tears, and smiles and many words of advice they left Bombay, supposedly freeing themselves of the constraints of our respective extended families. However with our arrival, they controlled us with those self same restrictive ropes.

Indians congregate wherever they find themselves. Within a short space of time, through family and community contacts, Mum and Dad were embraced by the North London Goan Association. They were invited to all the functions and by the time we were born they were stalwart members, serving on various committees. Though they both like to think of themselves as progressives, they would have liked X to come first but it was me. Having a boy as head of the family was something they were both familiar with. They both came from good Goan Catholic stock where sons were plentiful and certainly the leader of the pack. But the fact that I, Madhuri, named after my mother's favourite Indian film star, Madhuri Dixit, was the eldest was something they didn't have to contend with for long, as X was born a year later. This accounts for the fact that people assume we're twins. They also, always, and I mean always, assume that he's the eldest. In my youth, this was my albatross. I felt I had to set people straight as soon as they met us. But the older I got, the less I cared.

X and I were as close as two siblings can be: we fought and we made each other cry; we hugged, made up, laughed and started fighting all over again. But the dominant characteristic of our relationship was that we made each other laugh a lot because for a long time we had the same juvenile sense of humour. We didn't just know each other inside out; we were soulmates and allies against our parents and their demands. Although my feminist sensibilities balk when I think of it, one of my first memories of X was him coming to my rescue, and beating the hell out of another five year old at nursery. I can't for the life of me remember what the poor child did to make me cry, but as soon as X saw those tears, he launched in and pummelled the kid until the teacher pulled him off. He was my hero for all of two days before we started fighting again but my feelings for X were forever sealed after that, even if buried under the weight of sibling rivalry. We were always watching each other's back; stepping up to any challenge, here or in India where our cousins were always taking the mickey out of the way we looked or spoke.

From nursery we progressed onto the same primary and secondary schools where we gathered Avi, Babar, Carl, Madelena, and Francis. We were an eclectic crowd – Avi, an atheist because his parents were that rare breed of Indians who were hippies. People think of hippies as being white, Anglo Saxon, middle class drop outs. But, as we soon learnt, there were also Indians who fitted into that mould who had affluent parents so they had the resources to turn their back on expected professional occupations. Babar is a Muslim and had we not known him for as long as we did, you could have thought he was a fanatic from the devotion he steeped his words in and his irrevocable beliefs. Actually Babar is the gentlest soul, sensitive and caring of all the members of his family and his friends; always on the lookout for what they need. The most go-getting spirit was Carl, who from our primary school days, had mapped out a career for himself in the City and was determined from the age of eleven that this was for him. Madelena and Francis, also Catholics were, compared to me, tamer and more predictable until they showed their true colours. Since we had known each other from primary school, it was easy to slip into our proscribed roles, with Carl in charge, and the rest of us following. We named ourselves after no less a team than the Secret Seven. The numbers fitted, even if nothing else did; it was whimsical and made us feel we belonged- to what or why, we never troubled ourselves to find out.

By the time we were in our final years at St Stephen's, in Walthamstow, our paths were more or less mapped. Avi, taking after his parents was all set to take a few years off, no single gap year for Avi. His plans were to travel the globe and see the world. Babar had decided to do business studies to help support his family. Carl had his sights set on Oxbridge to read Mathematics, Madelena and Francis on London and Liverpool to read English and Anthropology respectively. X and I took the longest to decide. Like everyone else our parents' expectations weighed us down but we knew we had to choose for ourselves. It was easier knowing we had each others support. Neither of our choices offered us a secure future, and, not surprisingly, the parents were up in arms.

'What is the matter with you children?'

'Actually we are no longer children, Dad.' X looked across

at me and winked. This was his first shot at what, we anticipated, would be a searing mental doubles match that neither side felt they could loose.

'Son, I don't know where the two of you are living. You need skills, to find jobs, to earn a living.'

X tilted his head in my direction and I responded. 'Papa, human beings need to be able to look at ourselves and understand we are not alone and that we can learn from each other. Paintings are pictures of the world, and plays and acting give people the opportunity to think about the world we live in, and who we are.'

'Bravo, bravo.' X thumped me on the back almost causing me to slip.

Dialogues like this carried on throughout our final years.

On one occasion I remember Mum whispering to Dad, 'Let it be now. She'll never get in, so all the fuss will be for nothing'.

I was perfectly happy to let Mum give Dad plenty of false hope. When I got accepted they were both in a state of shock throughout the summer. I started in October and packed my rucksack each day, regularly attended lectures, and came home occasionally with bright coloured paintings and small sculptures which helped to calm their fears. My multi media work that was challenging and on occasions disturbing, I left at college.

I stood behind the kitchen door and listened as Mum spoke to Dad. 'She'll marry soon. Let her be, bas.' Though I saw that as another battle I'd have to fight, I was relieved that they had reconciled themselves to me going to St Martins. But Dad was not so easily placated as far as X was concerned.

'He should know better. He will have a family to look after. He needs a proper job. And none of this nonsense that he won't get in. These two are....'

I'm not sure what Dad was about to say but he stopped himself as I walked in. I pretended not to have heard and got on with helping Mum prepare dinner. When X walked in, Dad stood in front of him and said they had to talk. I sidled up next to X ready to add my two paisa.

'I want to talk to my son alone. Father and son. You stay here with your Mother.' His tone was abrasive and X sensed that Dad would only get more irate if I followed along, so he jerked his head which was enough for me to understand that I was to stay in the kitchen.

Mum and I pottered about not saying much. Both of us were trying to overhear what was being said particularly when the shouting started. It was X's final statement that stopped us in our tracks.

'I'm leaving this house and I mean it.'

'Go.'

I ran to the sitting room door that X pushed open, and tried to hold onto him, but he shoved me aside as he climbed the stairs to his room. I rushed after him, and watched as he threw his jeans and stuff into the case he used for our annual trips to India.

'You can't do this.'

'Mad' - bizarre though it sounds, he always called me that whenever he had something serious to say, 'I have to; otherwise I'll never get out.'

'We've always managed it before. We're a team.'

'Yeah but it's different for you. You know it is. But me? Let's face it, what good Goan family wants an unemployed actor for a son- in- law?'

'Not tonight. Not now.'

'No, I have to.'

'But where?'

'Listen, you can't tell Mum and Dad.'

'Don't be stupid, of course, I won't tell them.'

'I thought this might happen one day so I've been talking to Carl and his brother has a place that he rents out. He needs someone to look after it so I can have a room there as long as I take care of it and his tenants.'

'Where is it?'

'In Whitechapel.'

'That's miles away.'

'Don't be ridiculous.'

'But when will I see you?'

'Whenever you want. Here's the address and just make sure Mum and Dad never get hold of this.' X started scribbling on a piece of paper and shoved it into my pocket. When he'd packed his case and stuffed the rest of his things into his blue rucksack, he looked up at me. I was crying and he took me in his arms and held me tight before giving me a final hug.

'Listen, you know, I'll always be there for you. Don't worry. I'll be fine. It'll be the hardest on Mum but things'll calm down.'

'I want to come.'

'You can't – that would just be too much.'

If only I had held onto him or insisted on going with him or something perhaps things would have been different. But I just cried as he lugged his stuff downstairs. I followed him into the kitchen and watched him hold Mum.

'Have some food, son, before you go. Let me make you something to take.' Tears were trickling down her cheeks.

He shook his head.

'I love you Mum. You know that.'

Mum and I were both in floods but Dad was nowhere to be seen as X opened the front door and walked out onto the street. He was never to live at home again after that.

*

Mum had assumed I knew where he had gone to and I had to lie. She kept suggesting I ask his friends which I pretended to do always reporting back that no one knew. I tried to ease her pain by saying that X was sensible, and that once things had calmed down, he'd be in contact. In fact I met him once, sometimes twice a week, but most of the time, he was busy working. His focus was on getting a place at drama school. I was constantly encouraging him, though it wasn't entirely necessary, as he was running on his own steam which seemed to provide him with fuel enough to work long, and hard. I was very impressed

'Madelena told me Mum was at the school gate the other day so I had to wait until she'd left. I was nearly late for class.'

'X you can't blame her. She's worried sick about you.'

'I don't want to hurt her. I do, I feel bad. But Mad there's nothing I can do for now. If they know where I am, Dad'll start off again.'

'When are you going to tell them?'

'As soon as I get a place. I promise.'

It all felt so ridiculous but I understood the predicament X was in.

After X left, when Dad returned home from work, it was as though there was some kind of toxic odour that filled the house. We were barely able to breath let alone talk. This went on for months and was so suffocating that I suggested to Mum that I might share a place with another female student from college. She got worried and I heard her talking to Dad. On that occasion I didn't bother to eavesdrop on their conversation. But the result was that Dad returned to his old self or at least the noxious fumes eased off.

On Saturday 19th August 2000, I remember this date along with the others as clearly as though they were stamped on my forehead. We had just finished eating Mum's chicken biryani and I was about to clear the table when the doorbell rang. When I opened the door, I just stood there staring as though I was standing on a diving board. We hugged and didn't move until Mum shouted from the kitchen.

'Arre, who's there?'

X walked into the kitchen. Mum, of course held out her arms. Dad scrapped back his chair and stood up. I was frightened he was going to shout at X and tell him to get out.

'Wait. Please wait.' X put his hands to his lips.

'Don't start. Let him speak. He's our son. I want to hear what he's come to say.'

Dad sat back down again. X remained standing. I pulled up a chair next to him. 'I didn't want to hurt you both...

'Do you know how much ...?

'Bas.' Mum put up her hand to silence Dad.

'I didn't want to hurt you but at last I have good news to tell you. I have been offered a place at Royal Academy of Drama and Arts. It is one of the best drama colleges in England. People like Mark Rylance and Joely Richardson went there.

Mum and Dad clearly didn't recognise either of these names. I bit on my bottom lip and looked at X. He understood and started rattling off some Indian names which, in all honesty, I'd never heard of.

'Devika Rani, Habib Tanvir and Indira Varma.'

Mum and Dad's eyes began to follow X's words now.

'It is very difficult to get in. Every year hundreds of people are rejected. Anyway I have a place and a scholarship and will begin in September and I just wanted to let you know.'

I took hold of X's hand and was about to get up to give him the biggest hug but Mum beat me to it.

'I'm so proud, son. But the biryani's finished. Arre what can I give you?'

X laughed, 'Don't worry Mum I've already eaten. I just wanted to come over and let you know.'

X looked across at Dad who was still silent, still sitting stiff and upright.

'I just wanted to tell you.'

'So what now?' All our eyes turned to Dad. His tone was flat and it was difficult to gauge where he was coming from.

'Well I start in September.'

'You've already told us that.'

'If you mean will I come home. The answer is no. The place I have is convenient and I'm happy there.'

'So you don't intend to come home.'

'If you'll allow me, I'll come and see you and Mum regularly.'

'Of course, son. Please come.' Before Dad could even open his mouth, Mum had made the decision. This time I got up and hugged her and then hugged X. After a few moments Dad looked across at Mum and me and nodded.

Saturday 19th August 2000 remains a happy memory fixed in my mind unlike the subsequent dates, weeks and months that have left bitter, painful, permanent scars.

A year later, early Tuesday morning, on 19th November 2001, there was a hammering at the door as though it had been hit by lightning. I remember thinking I was dreaming.

When I opened my eyes, expecting silence, it was still continuing. I lay there for a minute wondering whether I should get up. Then I heard voices shouting, 'Open up.' I realised it wasn't a weekend-boozed-up idiot, but something more serious. By the time I got to the stairs, Dad was just opening the door.

A police officer stood there, pushing some card into Dad's face and edging his way in. He wanted X. Dad said he wasn't home. The officer raised his voice and stared at Dad.

'Mr Menezes if you don't assist us I'll arrest you for aiding and abetting. Do you understand?'

'Officer, I've just told you, he's not here.'

'Well then, where is he?'

X had decided not to give Mum and Dad his address but had promised Mum that he'd come round regularly which he did. For the past year we'd had lunch together pretty much every Sunday. Mum had got so used to the idea and Dad, in trying to patch up relations, had not pursued X for it, so they literally didn't know.

'I don't know.'

'You telling me that you don't know where your son lives?'

'Yes.'

'I'm warning you and this is the last time if you don't…'

'15 Whitechapel Avenue, Flat 5.'

Rubbing his chin, the officer turned around. 'And who might you be?'

'His sister.'

'So you know his address but your parents don't? I see.'

They had arrived at five in the morning and stayed hours. Mum got dressed with seconds of their entering the house. We all had to call to give our apologies to work and college, without explaining anything but fobbing people off with pathetic excuses. Men covered in white overalls arrived and started taking specimens from a variety of surfaces: the staircase, around the bathroom. Men went through X's old room with a fine toothcomb, emptying the cupboards, boxes, shelves. They took his old desktop that he hadn't used in years. We should have given it away but we certainly didn't want it taken away by the police. Dad kept asking what was going on but they all remained silent until they'd finished.

Finally around half eight in the morning, the officer who Dad had first spoken to told us all to sit down which we did in living room.

'Your son,' he said looking at Mum and Dad, 'your brother,' he said turning his head a fraction to look me straight in the eye, 'is accused of having raped a girl on Hampstead Heath and we are the investigating officers.'

My jaw just dropped.

'No, no, not my son. You are mistaken. Not my son.' Dad's voice was adamant and strong and spurred me on.

'You've got it wrong. It wasn't my brother. No way. Not my brother. I'm telling you now it's not my brother.'

'Whatever you may think, it is our job to investigate the crime. My colleagues will have gone round to your son's place and unless he has a rock solid alibi, he'll have been arrested by now.'

Shocked though we were by what this man was saying, we were all nevertheless certain that the truth would come out when they spoke to X. But everything happened so quickly after that visit. X was arrested. The victim was shown a photographic line up and pointed to X. Initially she said she thought it was him. Then when it got to Court, she pointed to X saying she was absolutely sure that he was the man who raped her. X was convicted, despite proclaiming his innocence in Court. Ma and I cried out to the jury that X wasn't guilty, that he hadn't and wouldn't commit rape. The judge sentenced him to 8 years. His lawyer appealed and when it was unsuccessful X and Ma and I were all screaming even louder and crying. By this stage Dad had ceased to attend the hearings. Mum and Dad were asked to resign from the North London Goan Association because people hinted what had happened had damaged the Association's reputation. Former friends and acquaintances kept their distance. Mum's tears were heard within the confines of the kitchen, occasionally when I was present, but most of the time, alone.

I went to visit him in Brixton Prison every week and with each visit he looked worse, more haggard like a man who had lived on the streets for decades, as thin as any refugee you see on telly, and frail like an old man.

The Secret Seven fell apart. Avi claimed his feminist politics meant that he couldn't take any other position than that of supporting the victim and set off on his travels. I've never heard from him since. Carl expressed his concern for our parents and me but kept his distance. Madelena and Francis never even contacted me or Mum and Dad and certainly weren't interested in seeing X. It was only Babar.

'I know X. He's like my brother. He wouldn't have, couldn't have. He's not that kind of a man.' Babar, like me, had a gut sense that X didn't rape the poor woman. I didn't blame her. In her distress she had mistaken X for the actual rapist. She didn't claim to know X and he certainly didn't know her. From every point of view it was appalling. Babar took time off from work, despite his family's disapproval and visited X in prison, and through the long months leading up to the trial, came to see Mum and Dad and me. When X's case finally reached the Crown Court, and then later the Appeal Court, Babar was there.

When I returned from a visit in July 2003 and told Babar how worried I was about X's physical and emotional well being he said we had to do something though neither of us knew what. He came back the following week and told me he had contacted a friend of a friend from The Haringey Gazette. He was an investigative journalist and after several discussions, Babar had convinced him to take on X's case. It was the best news we had received for over a year. We went together to Brixton to tell X. I don't know what I expected but his face was still. It was as though he'd been anaesthetized. Babar and I jabbered away about how this was such a positive development but X was silent throughout. By the time we left, it was as though we'd been talking to ourselves as X had said nothing.

Sometimes you only understand things in hindsight. That Thursday, 18th September 2003, X committed suicide. The Governor of Brixton Prison phoned in the small hours of the morning. I woke to Mum's howling. Dad remained cold and uninvolved and simply got on with what needed to be done. At X's funeral there was only us and Babar. Eight months later the journalist found the real rapist. The man confessed to not only this but twenty other counts of rape. X was cleared. Mum has never forgiven Dad and I don't think Dad will ever forgive himself.

You, in the Fading Light

Amna Khokher

I'm struggling to breathe: my kameez is too tight. I've squeezed into the silk dress, breasts protesting, desperate to break free. Mum smiles with satisfaction, nods her head as if that's what she wants – to hide my breasts, or tits, as Olivia would say, from the rest of the world.

'Perfect, isn't it perfect?' Mum cries, wrapping an orange chiffon dupata around my head. 'Aree, don't look yet.' She drapes a colossal necklace around my throat; Asian gold, it sits heavily against my chest.

'Nothing lighter?' I mutter, but she turns my body to face her mirrored wardrobe door.

'You see,' she says. 'I have wonderful taste, huh?'

I eye up my reflection. The gold-embroidered, tangerine salwar kameez shimmers back at me. My lips glisten like the inside of a peach. 'Great.'

She's beaming, standing there like some designer inspecting her work. Her daffodil-yellow salwar kameez is fitted on her slim body; a dupata is draped elegantly over one arm.

'You're now a woman, Sunita,' she says. 'Are you listening? Your tomboy days are gone. Understand?'

I clench my jaw. Just weeks ago I was sitting my final A-level exams and worrying about the spot on my cheek. I wasn't allowed to go out, drink alcohol, talk to boys – unlike my friends from school. Now I'm a woman ready for marriage?

Eyes and head dipped, I stare at the brown and beige swirls of the carpet and I understand. I understand why every Asian bride I've ever seen has stood this way, looking so fucking miserable.

Mum perches on the edge of her bed and pats the duvet beside her. I sit, keeping my distance.

'Listen carefully,' she says.

'I am listening.' I try to take a deep breath but the kameez is so tight it hurts my breasts. I hold my breath instead, refrain from screaming at her.

'Okay, okay.' She sighs and places her hand on my leg. 'Your wedding night is approaching,' she says, an eyebrow arching up.

I squeal in protest and bat her hand off my leg. 'Seriously, please –'

'Ah, choop. Quiet. It's my duty to talk to you about s-e-x. Such an important part of marriage, betee: it's the glue that holds a couple together.' She brings the tips of her forefingers together in front of my face. 'Glue,' she repeats.

Sick. I'm going to be sick. I try to drown out her voice. I focus on how it will be afterwards, when the wedding's over. I'll be free from their restrictions. I'll wear sleeveless dresses and eat salmon with boiled potatoes like I do at Olivia's. I'll go to parties and sleep when I please. Maybe Suneel will let me attend art classes and won't think they're a waste of time like Mum and Dad do.

'There will be times when you don't feel like doing it,' Mum continues, 'but a wife's duty is to satisfy her husband. We must to keep them... faithful.'

I close my eyes and rub my temples, but she flicks my hand off my face and slaps my wrist.

'I'm telling you these things for your own good. You're not a child anymore.'

Not a child anymore – so everyone keeps telling me.

*

Two weeks earlier Olivia and I sat on the swings behind her house. I'd just told her my parents had arranged my marriage. The afternoon sunshine illuminated her green eyes and yellow hair and her eyes filled. She hooked her little finger into her mouth and bit it, the way she does when she wants to say something but is trying not to. Then she sat on her hands.

'You're not a kid anymore,' she said. 'They can't tell you what to do. You've got to stand up to them.'

I shook my head. 'I've tried. Trust me.'

I didn't tell her about the fights, about how I begged Mum and Dad to let me go to university first. Mum explaining that this was the way it had always been, Mum, her mum before that, and hers before that, always marrying as soon as they reached womanhood. 'What did you expect?' Mum had asked. 'And why don't you want to? Is there someone else?' Her lips twisted in disgust. 'Chi, chi, chi – a boyfriend?' She looked at Dad and started sobbing. She said they would disown me if I dishonoured them. I tried to bribe them, promising to cook and clean every day, to become their slave, but even that didn't sway them. 'Marriage means being settled, betee,' Dad said. 'And we want to see you settled.'

I didn't tell Olivia all this because I wanted to appear as together and cool as she was. 'It's my culture,' I said, trying to sound wise. 'My fate.'

Olivia shook her head. 'I'll run down the aisle and kidnap you if I have to.'

My eyes stung. 'And then what?' I said, more abruptly than I intended. I looked away and dug my forehead against the metal chain of the swing.

'Hey,' she said. 'It'll be okay.'

I looked back at her and she smiled kindly, her teeth perfectly straight, beautiful like every part of her.

'Listen, stay over tonight,' she said, her voice still soft. 'Mum's working.'

I nodded. She was the only English friend I was allowed to stay with because our families had known each other so long, and it would be such a relief to get away. 'I'll pop home and get my stuff.'

*

Satisfied with the way I look, Mum leaves her bedroom, instructing me to come down shortly after her. Downstairs, the hallway is empty. I look around, searching for somebody, anybody. There's a cheer from the living room and the drum of the dolki fills the corridor. It shudders through my whole body – boom-boom, boom-boom. I walk towards the living room in a trance, wondering if Olivia is there.

The door swings open as I reach it. Hands pull me in. The room is alive with music and clapping. Various shades of yellow blur together as I'm showered in confetti. Flower necklaces are draped around my neck. It's everything a bride-to-be would expect a week before the wedding, at her mehendi, but I don't know how to act. Should I greet people or smile for the cameras that are flashing around me?

Hands guide me to a tinsel-draped chair at the end of the room. It's only when I feel the lips against my forehead and smell the minty aftershave that I realise they are Dad's hands. I peer up at him and he places his hand on top of my head and then touches my cheek, exactly as he did when I got straight As in my GCSEs. Then Mum pulls him away by the arm, complaining about the tandoori chicken being too hot, as if he has some magic potion to dampen the spice.

I look for Olivia but I can't see her in the crowd. Finally, I turn to face Saneel, who's sitting beside me in a similarly decorated chair. I force a smile.

*

When I returned to Olivia's with my toothbrush and pyjamas, her mum had already left for work. Olivia drew the living room curtains although it wasn't yet dark.

'Look,' she said, flicking on the lamp. 'What are you going to do?'

'I have to go through with it,' I told her. 'Too many people to keep happy. Mum, Dad, Nano; aunts, uncles, Saneel's family. I'm trapped.'

She sat beside me on the sofa. 'It's so unfair.'

I felt tears stirring in my throat again but I swallowed hard to thrust them down. What would crying achieve? 'It's always been expected of me. I've always known.'

Olivia squeezed a cushion against her chest. 'You ever been in love?'

I saw her swallow, and I kept my eyes on her throat for a moment before looking up to her eyes. 'I think so.'

She smiled and hooked her small finger into her mouth. Bit it gently. 'Shall I make us hot chocolate?' she asked.

*

Saneel leans towards me. I can smell his aftershave, strong and sweet. 'Look at you!' he says.

I've always been close to Saneel. We played together as kids – me on my BMX, him on his skateboard. During our GCSEs I helped him with physics and he taught me about poetry. We're like brother and sister.

I roll my eyes. 'I look like a bloody Christmas tree.'

He laughs. He looks odd in kurtha salwar. Like a little boy, in his father's clothes. But his hair is spiked up with gel as usual, like this is any other normal day.

'You look bloody ridiculous too,' I tell him.

He laughs again, but this time it's a nervous kind of laugh, and he leans back into his chair.

I carefully scan the room. It's split, women mingling amongst women, men amongst men. It was Mum's idea to have a joint mehendi, men and women all in one room. 'Very modern,' she said. That made me laugh. Traditional when it suited her, modern when she wanted, switching herself on and off whenever the mood took her. That's why she'd insisted I wear bright orange instead of traditional yellow, too. Modern, very modern.

I look and look but I do not see her. She is not here. Olivia is not here.

In the middle of the room my young cousins, dressed in matching lemon-yellow lengas, are beginning a dance. Their long skirts swish against the floor as they circle each other. They clap in time to the beat of the dolki and start singing – something about weddings and brides, wishing happiness and everlasting joy. It's like a chant, as if they are casting a spell.

My eyes flit around the room. From the corner of my eye, I can see the girls bending down and picking up thick wooden sticks painted in bright colours. They hit the sticks against each other as they dance: clack, clack, clack. I'm drawn back to them.

Olivia is not here.

As I watch their faces, stern with concentration, I imagine running out of the room and down the street. I picture myself banging on Olivia's door. And then, as I've fantasised so many times before, I see Olivia and me catching a train to a new city. But as I picture bustling streets and high-rises, my aunts crowd around me, and the image vanishes.

*

Olivia returned with two blue mugs of hot chocolate with tiny marshmallows floating on top. She looked very serious as she handed me a mug and sat down.

'You can't go through with it,' she said, sliding her hand across the sofa until it touched mine. 'You know what you really want.'

Her voice was all air, and I felt relief so deep I wanted to cry. For years we'd flirted back and forth, but I often thought I'd imagined it. Other times I questioned my feelings, thought maybe I did fancy Leo Thomas from my class, who had dark hair and piercing blue eyes. Girls swooned over him, but I never felt nervous around him, or worried about my hair being a mess or my nose being too big, like I did around Olivia.

'I'll confront your parents with you,' Olivia said, her eyes bright.

'Forget them.' There was only the tiniest hint of nerves in my voice. 'I don't want to talk about them.'

She nodded. 'Neither do I.'

In the bedroom, she forgot to do up the curtains. She undid the buttons of her shirt first. It floated to the floor. I was slow although everything inside me was racing – heart, mind, the pulse in my stomach. Finally, I peeled off my jeans and lay down on the bed in my T-shirt.

Olivia's breath was warm against my neck as her body moulded to mine. Her fingers were silky, smooth, pulling my T-shirt off in one quick move, and trailing the length of my neck, the space between my breasts, the curve of my stomach. It felt like she'd done it before, but I knew she hadn't. I knew her.

I relaxed then, as her body arched over mine and her green eyes shimmered like a fox's. I touched the freckle above her right breast.

'Birth mark?' I asked.

She grinned. 'Right on my tit.'

*

When my cousins' dancing comes to an end, my aunts gather around me. All smiles, they grab pieces of mitai and shove them into my mouth. The buttery candy chokes me. Someone presses a glass of water against my lips and I sip. Reassured that I've recovered, the next woman holds a ball of gulab jamun to my mouth. I bite into the brown syrupy sponge. As more and more mitai is forced into my mouth, I focus my eyes on the ground. I chew and swallow, chew and swallow. My heart sinks lower, lower, lower. Olivia is not here, but everyone else is.

*

Afterwards, Olivia and I lay beneath the sheets, looking at each other. The daylight was fading and she had lit a candle.

'I can't believe this,' I said.

She sat up, swung her legs over the side of the bed, and reached for a cigarette from her bedside table. She lit it with the candle, breathed in, out.

'I… you know. Love. And you,' she said without looking at me.

In that moment, being with her, naked, in the fading light, felt like the most natural thing in the world. More real than anything I'd ever experienced, and more dream-like.

'Me too,' I said.

She turned to face me. Smoke curled around her hair. 'Don't get married,' she whispered. 'Let's go to university, get a place to share, like we always talked about. We'll cook ratatouille in the evenings. Play jazz and paint on weekends.'

I wanted to cry, but I forced myself to swallow. 'I can't. You know I can't.'

She looked away. 'Can't or won't?'

I wanted to ask her what we would live on. And what we would do afterwards. I could never tell my family. I'd be better off running away with a man. I would be flicked away like dirt. Erased. 'Can't.'

She stood up and covered herself with her silk dressing gown that was draped over a chair. She stood with her back to me, looking out the window.

'So what was this?' she said. 'Just a fuck. A cheap shag?'

My chest tightened. I wanted to get up and hold her, but I

suddenly felt too naked. I pulled the bed covers tight around me. 'It's not like that,' I said, my voice thick. 'You know that.'

She pressed her forehead against the window and banged it against the glass, hard, three times. 'I know, I know,' she said, and it sounded like she was crying, too. 'I know.'

*

I smell her before I see her. Flowers. Musk. I look up and my face meets hers as she kneels in front of me. She is wearing a pale yellow dress that reaches the floor; a golden cardigan is draped across her shoulders and her hair is pinned up, showing off her slender neck. My breath catches in my throat.

She picks out a small pink ball of mitai and gently pushes it into my mouth. Her fingers linger against my lips; I close my eyes and send a prayer of thanks to the world, the universe, whoever sent her into my life.

She removes her fingers, licks them clean.

'You look beautiful,' I say, swallowing all the other things I want to say. Don't ever leave me, even when I'm married; remember when we were eleven and we stole a cigarette from your dad's drinks cabinet and swore not to tell anyone? It'll be like that.

She leans in to hug me. I breathe into her neck. My tight kameez presses against my chest, which is bursting with emotions I have no names for, and the kameez tears beneath my armpit. But I don't care about the rip, because she is here, and I breathe a little freer as I picture us later. I imagine me lifting my arms so she can take off my kameez; I imagine breathing freely in her embrace when the house is asleep.

But she lets go too soon. 'Good bye, Sunita,' she whispers. Her eyes fill as she presses her hand against mine, and she stands and walks away before I manage to speak.

She glides through the crowd and out through the door. I want to shout: you can't go; you can't leave me. But she has already left.

Someone shoves another piece of mitai into my mouth and I choke on it, spluttering and coughing. Tears drip down my face.

'Don't cry, betee,' Aunty Yasmin says. 'You're not going far.'

I peer up at her and at other smiling aunts. My grandmother is dancing gingerly in the middle of the room, hands raised in celebration. Dad is hugging an old friend. I look over at Saneel; he is shaking his brother's hand. He laughs, and it's deep and dreadful.

A wail escapes me. I dry my eyes with my dupata. I dab and dab and dab. I tell myself that at least I will always have this: Olivia, in the cool and fading light; my Olivia, bare and beautiful and bright.

The Owl

Reetinder Boparai

Every morning, Mrs Ananda Chowdary woke up and bathed herself before conducting morning prayers giving offerings to the goddess Lakshmi. Mrs C kept her house clean and so Hari the servant was always busy. She stood behind him pointing out any miniscule of dust that had been missed saying, 'Wipe that dust or be it on your head if Lakshmi leaves.' Lakshmi, the goddess of fortune and wealth, didn't reside in filthy homes, so Mrs C would end her instructions by saying, 'No money- no job.' Hari, who had a growing family, took to wiping the household surfaces twice or thrice a day.

'Hari, Hari, bring me my breakfast in the conservatory,' shouted Mrs C as she passed the kitchen on her way to the warmth of the morning sun to sooth her arthritic joints. But on entering the conservatory she shuddered on finding the bamboo blinds drawn and the room in darkness. 'Hari!' she shouted. Grabbing the drawstring to the blind, she mumbled under her breath, 'Why is the room not prepared?' The blind clunked rolling on itself allowing light to gradually sweep up from the depths of the room and work its warm magic up Mrs C's body, but on touching her face she heard a flutter from behind. As the fan was off, she put the malfunction in her hearing down to her tinnitus which for her was caused by too much wax, so she made a mental note to apply some warm mustard oil in her ears at night.

Mrs C turned around into the room, but instead of reclining on her rosewood sofa she stood frozen to the spot on seeing a feathered creature swoop from the ceiling. Mrs C screamed. The animal fell with a thud onto the sofa, while a few loose feathers hung in the air before they floated back down onto the owl. Mrs C shrieked, 'Hari!' Cutlery and crockery rattled in the corridor while the animal tried hoisting itself up.

'Madam, madam,' said Hari, in the doorway, with a tray of potato parathas and yoghurt. 'Save yourself Madam!' However, Mrs C stood rooted with eyes fixed on the owl that was still flapping.

She was only drawn from this state by her husband's footsteps resonating on the marble slabs along the corridor at an unusually faster pace than normal. He entered the room still in his pyjamas and pushing back his white dishevelled hair from his brow revealing dark circled eyes he said, 'You've frightened him.'

Redness shot into Mrs C's cheeks and she raised her finger at him as he retrieved his bird and she uttered, 'That's a deadly beast.'

But her husband stroked the bird whose eyes, resembling two dark pools stared back at Mrs C. 'Hari, close the blinds; the poor animal is being blinded by all this daylight,' said Mr C. Hari moved over to the window.

'No leave them,' she said. 'This is my conservatory Mr Chowdary; take that beast to the coops.'

'This is our conservatory.'

'What? Mr Chowdary put him in the coops with the rest of his kind. You know the rule – no owls in this house.'

'No, this young bird is injured' - he gently stretched out the bird's left wing – 'and look he's lost some feathers.' In response the bird closed his eyes and pulled the wing back into the safety of his body. 'Poor soul; don't you worry your feathers will grow back.' And turning to his wife, Mr C said, 'He'll stay here till he's able to fly.'

Her words became trapped as her anger rose up within her. Mr C continued, 'Don't you see he's different? He's a pure white owl and such creatures bring good fortune. Ananda, my dear, your goddess Lakshmi who you worship rides on such a creature.'

'Hari, pack my belongings!' But before marching from the room she turned to her husband and said, 'You're sending me away just like you sent my son away.'

He shook his head. 'Rahul took the job abroad for the opportunities.'

'What's so good him being a doctor in England when I need him here? Look at me!' She lifted her disfigured arthritic hand. 'It was your dream to go to England not your son's. I'll be in the annex until you see sense and send that owl where it belongs.' She shook her head knowing that an owl in the house, no matter what shade, was trouble. And so that afternoon Mrs C led Hari who carried her belongings:

the rope bed, clothes and the Lakshmi statue out of the house.

No white, grey, black or brown owl could disguise that call. The eerie sounds, in the night, had sent her in a whirl when she arrived as a young bride to the house. The creatures nesting in the conservatory had kept her awake night after night and she, in her delirium, had sent the doctor's sedatives flying, fearing death would take her in her sleep, and so she had become nocturnal like the owls staying awake ensuring the ghostly echoes didn't whisk her away before she had mothered a child. She took refuge one night in the out house – the annex- and stayed there till her husband saw sense and built the coops for his beloved owls on the edge of their land by the wheat field where they remained content hunting the small creatures that took sanctuary amongst the crop. They had remained there for four decades, while she slept with cotton wool in her ears to guard against the calls of death.

From the annex, she watched until Mr C drew the blinds in the morning so his owl could sleep, but this didn't deter her vigilance as during the course of the day Hari became her eyes and ears. Hari brought news of Mr C laying mouse traps for Ronack's night time meal or Mr C was busy washing Ronack's special blanket or master and bird were snoozing in the conservatory, and he finished his reports by telling her the state of her rosewood sofa, which was becoming overridden with claw marks. Under different circumstances, she would have asked Hari to shift it, but she didn't want Mr C to know she was watching, for he may presume she was concerned.

Each night with Hari gone, Mrs C took up her position by the window's edge, hidden from an outsider's gaze, to observe Mr C open the conservatory door and pull up the blinds to let the darkness in. She knew her husband was encouraging the owl to take flight in order to build up strength in his wings, but the stupid bird just stood on his perch.

Of course, monitoring the owl and her husband didn't relieve Hari from cleaning the house and Mrs C requiring up-to-date cleanliness reports to allay her fears for deserting her husband and leaving him vulnerable to the owl. And the matter wasn't helped when Hari after mopping the kitchen floor one morning barged into the annex and said, 'Master's received some bad news.'

Mrs C was silent, so Hari continued, 'The shares have dropped in price.' Hairs stood to attention on the back of Mrs C's arms, even though it was not less than 40 degrees Celsius. It was happening – her suspicions about that owl were coming true.

'Madam you need to come - he's just staring at the letter.'
'What's the loss?'
'He didn't say.'

'Ronack isn't the white owl of Lakshmi,' said Mrs C knowing she had made the situation worse by taking Lakshmi from the house. She told Hari to mop the whole house, which included the kitchen a second time, and to inform her when he had finished, so she could offer extra prayers to Lakshmi before the day was over. What else could she do? She couldn't go back with Ronack still in residence.

At night Mrs C, tired from a despondent mind that had recounted countless prayers, settled by the annex window to monitor the pair in the conservatory. Although she was on watch, Mrs C allowed herself the odd snooze because all nights were alike where Mr C remained asleep on the rosewood sofa beside Ronack who stood on his perch till dawn. But around midnight, having only snoozed for half an hour, Mrs C awoke to the tail end of a rasping sound. She jerked forward to discover the image in the conservatory had altered, for no longer were master and bird together as only Mr C lay asleep - the bird had vanished.

Creeping into the night, yet keeping within the annex's shadow, Mrs C was surrounded by silence interrupted only by the gentle rustle of the wheat. As she stood surveying the glistening field under the night's spotlight, she caught in the distance a cloaked creature exit the forest; Mrs C fell back against the annex's wall. The serrated brickwork didn't affect Mrs C's dorsal skin as she pushed back to escape from the apparition encroaching forward sucking the glimmer from the landscape.

A voice shouted, 'No,' freed her from the trance and she spotted Mr C run into the field. Ronack flapped fumbling low over the wheat field; Mr C swung his arms to catch his bird only for it to shoot up into the night sky. Though she thought him a fool, for chasing a bird, she didn't reprimand him and tell him to come back. How could she when they weren't talking? The bird hovered over Mr C, while he cupped his hands saying, 'Come down.' In response Ronack did come down, but instead of landing in his master's hands he zoomed past and headed for the forest looming in the distance. 'Come back – you are too weak to leave!' he shouted and without looking back at his wife or his house, Mr C in his pyjamas and blue rubber flip flops went in pursuit of his bird.

***

Mrs C lay alone in the dark and pulled out her ear plugs. Silence, there was nothing but the clock ticking on the bed side table displaying five minutes until the midnight hour. She walked over to the French doors and parted the curtains. She looked out over the fallow field, which had remained so for a number of years; nothing took root in its soil since Mr C passed away. A halo like mist hung above the dark earth. The estate was desolate but for Hari and his family having taken up residence in the annex. Each morning he would diligently dust and clean, although due to his years when she complained of the dust he replied, 'Madam that is not dust but the white in your eyes.'

Near the conservatory, she noticed a shadow steal past. Mrs C locked the French doors. She put back the cotton plugs tightly in her ears. Mrs C sat on her bed with her chin on her knees and rocked. And then it began – the screech – 'Eeeee.. Ananda!' She pressed her hands tightly over her ears, but that didn't block the scraping on the conservatory roof. Ananda's teeth clenched and she darted into the bathroom where there were no windows. She clung to the shower curtain trying to make no noise, but her arms were shaking and the rings on the curtain were clanging together.

It was the same each night and at first she had thought it a dream, though her wakefulness denied her such solace. She sat in the bathroom, night after night, not looking at the creature outside. She was certain he would swallow her away from this life. Sleep had eluded her again and she sat awake till the sun rose in case sleep with its darkness took her away.

Mr C's feet had pointed south on the funeral pyre, so he could walk with the dead. Hari had stood back with Mrs C, while Rahul lit his father's pyre and the fire had burned high over Mr C consuming his body till it was no more. They had taken his ashes and freed him in the river to let his soul transcend this world.

He had gone and she was alone, but for the visitor with its disturbing calls had drawn her back to when she had first arrived in the house. On the phone, she had pleaded with Rahul to come home and capture the creature and he had said, 'Ma, I'll be coming, in a couple of weeks.' She had waited and the couple of weeks had transpired into months and years, and still he didn't come. And so she just waited for the sun to rise and for the creature to go.

She sat in the bathroom waiting for the nightmare to pass and it did each dawn. She waited for the night when the stillness would visit her and Mr C would be lying beside her again. She had so much to say: she should have stayed, she should have protected him from his folly, she should have insisted he got rid of the owl. She knew it was not too long to wait.

The day after Mr C had disappeared she had sat listening to the whirring of a fan and had tried to concentrate on the inspector's words.

'Madam, can I get you tea?'

She nodded to his words hoping if she did it would all sink in.

'We found your husband Madam. We think a truck hit him.' She sat with the thought of a truck and Mr C.

The inspector carried on, 'No one saw the driver; it was late at night.' He slowly closed the file, but before putting it aside he asked, 'Madam what was he doing in his night clothes so far from home? Was he visiting someone?'

A tear had fallen from her eye at the insinuation the inspector was making about Mr C's character.

'Madam, did you and your husband have any difficulties?'

She shook her head saying, 'No we were happy.'

Tears had fallen over the years knowing if she had stayed in the house it would have been different: Mr C would still be alive and she would not have been left alone. And now the eyes were dry and she waited for the sun to rise and for the creature to sleep. Ronack was searching for his master and had grown strong with his missing wing feathers having grown back grey.

She sat knowing Mr C had been too quick to believe Ronack had been a true white owl.

Nine

Nilopar Uddin

'Stay near Mummy,' the woman called out. The child she addressed was crouching a few yards away, shivering in the Cornish breeze.

'It's baby turtle Mama!' the child jumped up to look back at her mother, her face sliced in half by a toothy grin.

The woman walked over to her daughter and crouched down to peer at the creature, pleased at how powdery soft its gently pointed face looked.

'It's a tortoise, baby.' She picked it up gingerly, her pulse racing a little. She was not an animal person generally. She set it down as gently as she could on the grassy knoll and then taking the child's hand, she led them back to the car.

'Why did you do that Mama? Maybe he doesn't want to be on the grass.'

'He'll be safer there, away from the cars, the woman replied, pressing the child's hand against her thigh, willing her to stay put. The child, distracted, asked her something else, and the woman, busy loading the car boot with the suitcases, did not reply. Above them, the cerulean sky swept a smattering of clouds out into the horizon. Behind them, the craggy silver edges of the Fowey estuary glinted.

The brakes of a car screamed behind her, and even before she turned, even before she beheld the collision of that sharp white bonnet against the nimble frame of her barely-there child, an old fear re-claimed her. It re-possessed her. It clamped down on her throat so she could emit only a feeble yelp, not the lung-ripping roar she wanted to let out. She stumbled to her child, blind to every colour and hue except the tart scarlet against the black tarmac. She heard the driver pleading something, and she heard other voices beyond that. But these sounds seemed not to rouse this limp body in her arms.

She'd never known this child to be so still: from utero to the world, this child had come to her, chipper, spirited, always, always smiling. This body, pale and still, could not be that child.

§

Nine was the age I spotted a mud stain in the lining of my underwear.

When I saw it again, smeared against the fresh new pair I had put on, I did that imaginative leap that children are so capable of doing – from sensible sanity, I fled to nightmarish and unaccountable terror. In a moment, I was convinced that bleeding from this unknown place meant certain death and needing to convey this dread to someone, I ran out to Baba, bypassing Mummy cleaning the lunch dishes in the kitchen. I held the soiled item inches from his face and shrieked incomprehensibly.

Mummy materialised and within moments realised what had happened. She snatched my stained underwear away from where I held them, unhygienically inches from Baba's nose, and she tried to explain in soothing murmurs that it was just my period, which I had started earlier than she had expected. This explanation did absolutely nothing for me, because even in the precocious eighties, nine was a little early for the state to dispense sex education through the school system. It also did little to assuage Baba's terror, as he refused to believe that a nine year old was capable, physically, of menstruating. After she reassured him that it was indeed early, but possible, it occurred to him that his baby daughter was no longer a baby, and that fact, I think, terrified him more. He lashed out at Mummy, reprimanding her for not preparing me for this day, and my hysteria heightened: I thought that this period must be a long-concealed fatal illness that had loomed over me since birth and come to claim me early.

My hysteria however was nothing compared to my parents' sudden anger. Mummy retaliated that holding down a full time job as a hospital nurse and a mother of two didn't leave room for chit-chats, and if my father wasn't such a backward Indian, he could have informed me himself, on one of the many days that he was home 'looking for work'. She said these latter three words with such barely concealed sarcasm and derision that Baba bristled immediately. I very clearly remember the specks of greying stubble on his jaw line quiver as he swallowed hard. Ostensibly, Baba took offence at the word 'backward', reminding my mother that the very fact that she had a job when she didn't need to work was a sign of a progressive and supportive husband, and that he would not hear such racist stereotyping in front of his children. Mummy, who by then was beginning to regret saying it, balked that he should not appreciate the gravity of their financial situation, teetering as it was, on the periphery on her meagre salary, and her eyes reddened with tears at the suggestion that she might be racist. She then shouted a naughty word, which I stopped crying to listen to.

Then I watched on, silent, open-mouthed, as the two of them began to push each other. When did their pushes become shoves? Their shoves change to slaps? Their slaps turn to punches? I don't remember, but I do remember that soon, as I stood whimpering in the middle of the room, Mummy and Baba, conducting this jarring, violent dance around me, became a mess of limbs and screams and blood and tears, and I crouched down and sank my head into my elbows and stayed there until it ended.

It ended with a severely broken nose, and Mummy, her right eye swollen almost to a close, explaining the niceties of putting on a sanitary towel in the hospital toilets, as Baba waited to be seen by the A&E doctor. Thus was ushered in a fortnight of exile for Baba, months of iciness upon his return, and a sleeping bag that lay splayed like a crime investigation's chalk outline on my brother's floor where Baba slept for what felt like an eternity. And it was all my fault or as my brother loved to remind me, the fault of my stupid bloody knickers.

Nine was the age that Baba sat atop his steel trunk, stuffed to the brim with items that were wholly inappropriate for the cold climate he was destined for: Bata flip-flops, a plastic container of purple molasses, and several sets of flimsy cotton kurta pyjamas with machine-sewn embroidery. With these items in tow, his parents sent him off into the big wide world that was England. To claim his fortune. And, I suppose they hoped theirs too.

I imagined Baba embarking on this journey because imagination was all I had, as he refused to talk about his life before he met my mother. For him life hadn't begun until he saw her blond hair dipping in and out of the River Dee one March morning. He said he thought she was demented, emphasising the d and t in the ways that Bangladeshi native speakers do. He liked to point out, that while Mummy swam in her underwear (Mummy swore it was a swim suit), he was wearing three layers, and a hat. Life before that March morning was a lovely grey abyss which my imagination could freely colour and decorate as it pleased. I imagined he boarded something exotic, perhaps a glass submarine, and that it remained under water for many years until the vessel surfaced in the grey English Channel. I imagined him befriending sea horses radiating fairy dust and chattering dolphins and ethereal jelly fish that floated by before his very eyes. I imagined his legendary stoicism being born and matured during this journey under the stern and stentorian eye of the submarine's Captain, who must have resembled, as all Captains surely did, Captain Picard from Star Trek's

Next Generation. I imagined him suffering at first from the welded brunt of both homesickness and seasickness, and the pain fading slowly in the face of his audacious curiosity at the foreignness around him - the wonders of marine life and the manners and habits of the Englishmen that made up the crew.

Truth be told, I didn't even know what mode of transport he took to arrive in England. In fact, my knowledge of his exile was only gleaned from the rants of a manic depressive great aunty, who, on one of her visits, fell sick. This episode, coincided with (or perhaps was even caused by) my grandparents' annual visit.

'You cruel woman,' her voice was so shrill, that my brother and I, spraying each other with water from the garden hose, ran around the back of the house to the patio where our great aunt was taking tea with our grandmother.

'You cruel, greedy woman!'

Mummy and our great uncle appeared behind us, and held us by our shoulders, as though we were the ones about to make an attack.

'Sending your nine year old baby – nine years old! – you send him halfway around the world to be a slave so you can wear your fine benarasi silks!'

Our great uncle rushed into the house to fetch his wife's medicine, and Mummy watched my grandmother who continued to chew on a pastry and who then proceeded to pick up a tea spoon to stir her tea. All of us flinched at this nonchalance, and it only enraged my great aunt all the more.

'You eat his flesh, you drink his tears, you monstrous woman!' My great aunt slammed her heavily-ornamented hand down on the iron patio table, and the tea things rattled with fear. 'Making him work in a restaurant! At that age? What are you? A Monster!'

For nights afterwards, I would have nightmares of a stern elderly lady, her hair clipped in a tight bun, wandering the earth nibbling young flesh and stirring infants' tears into her black tea.

Often when I met nine or ten year olds, I visualized Baba of that height and build, and found myself marvelling how little he'd been. I pushed children of that age - generally our neighbour Maurice and my cousin Chandu - to do a chore just so I could imagine how my nine year old Baba would have looked, pushing a broom, cleaning a glass, washing a plate, or standing on a stool. For my brother's birthday, my parents allowed him to have Chandu, Maurice and some of his friends to stay for a sleepover. I challenged them to stand in the rain in their pyjamas, to see who could last the longest. Boys will do anything in the name of winning a dare. But really my objective was to picture how little boys looked when they stood outside on a cold, wet English night clothed in thin cotton, just as Baba would have stood shivering by an open kitchen door in the restaurant.

Could I send off my nine year old to an alien land with alien guardians aboard an alien ship? Did it require a deft courage or a selfish delusion?

These questions plagued my relationship with my grandparents. After my brother and I were born, my grandparents expressed their urgent desire to meet us. And thus began their annual visits. Mummy would observe that they were more interested in everything English but us. I grew up wary of their arrivals as the gentle spring faded and the moody summers loomed. Even in the heat of August, their visits lowered the temperature in our home to an almost wintry cool. They pinched our cheeks now and again, asked us, with feigned interest about what we studied, and gushed at my mother's rather poor culinary skills. Baba smiled through it all, but it was a smile that didn't pull down the outer corners of his eyes like his real smile did. I sensed something amiss and searched and searched for some presence of anger or awkwardness in him, though I found none. I was too young to realise that it should have been an absence of something that I ought to have searched for- an absence of a genuine affection between parent and child. The presence of my grandparents made me moody and long faced. I once heard Mummy giggling on the phone that I sat like a protective dog by Baba's side and glowered at them through many of their visits.

My daughter sits where I used to sit now, though she is a different onlooker than I had been at her age. She is one step removed and can observe their interactions without the disapproval that bristled my brows. She smilingly takes salty pakoras my grandmother offers to her, whilst curiously watching Baba's benign gaze and complacent nods imitating the nonchalance visible in my grandparents' own expressions.

'Mama,' She cocked her head in the drive back from one of these visits, 'When Maya cuts her knee, what does Mama do?' She had taken to referring to herself in the third person and this made her sound, to me anyway, like a child Siddartha, on the verge of enlightenment.

'Well,' I said moving up a gear, 'I would clean your cut, and put on a Micky Mouse Plaster.'

'And?' Maya insisted, willing me with raised brows as a teacher would to encourage a child who should know the answer. I hesitated.

'What would Mama do to make Maya get better faster?' Maya repeated with exaggerated patience.

'I would give your knee the miracle kiss!' I laughed, relieved to have found the answer and entertained by her precociousness.

'Yes.' Maya was silent a moment, looking ahead of her. Her head was cocked and she was picking at the skin of her forefinger, so I knew she hadn't finished.

'When Nanabhai had his faint today...'

'Fainted,' I corrected, 'Nanabhai did not have a faint, he fainted...because of his diabetes, it's nothing to worry about Mayoo, we've talked about this...'

'Mama, stop talking Mama!' Often I went off on a tangent, and often I was rebuked.

'Sorry baba, go on.'

'Well when Nanabhai fainted today,' She emphasised it a

little sarcastically, 'His Mama didn't give him a miracle kiss!'

It was true. Baba had been suffering from low blood pressure and diabetes for a few years now, and as a result he sometimes lost consciousness briefly. He had fainted this afternoon in the presence of Maya and his mother, and when I ran into the room, hearing Maya shouting for me, I found her crouched with Baba on the floor, and hovering above them was his mother. My grandmother stood aloof, her arms crossed, with the air of a passerby looking in on an accident happening on the road she was walking on. My grandfather was on the edge of the sofa where he had been perched peering with some concern at the scene, but not concerned enough to actually get up. It was utterly unfathomable to me. Maya, as a child who was, (much to my husband's disdain), being brought up within the strict confines of attachment parenting, was equally dumbfounded. It was to us both, eerie and abnormal. Baba's estrangement at nine seemed to have amputated that phantom umbilical cord that attaches a child to its parents long after the midwife concludes her clamping and cutting of the physiological cord.

Nine was the age Mummy realized that morning dew was not the residue of rainy nights. She discovered this from being woken abruptly around midnight by the loud bang of the front door as her father left and then being kept awake by the muffled sobs of her mother. Mummy couldn't fall asleep again, and those sobs clanged against her heart strings throughout the night. She recounted once that she had wished for a thunder storm or even some gentle drizzle to shift the sadness that engulfed their home that night. But there was no such help from the barren night sky and those lone sobs throbbing from her mother's room threw punches at Mummy's heart, keeping sleep at bay, making her feel bruised with fear and sorrow, relentlessly, until dawn gleamed beneath the curtains and she rose to dress for school.

She made her own breakfast that morning, and took her dish to an empty table to eat alone: she was an only child who, for the first time, realised that to be an only child meant to be without a sibling at a time when one would have been so comforting. Mummy was surprised when she closed the door behind her and found dewdrops glistening on the neglected lawn. She walked to school crying silently into the morning air, her toes in her summer sandals damp from the dew on the grass, arms crossed over her chest, fingers clawing at the insides of her elbows.

On the inside of Mummy's elbows, the skin is dark and calloused. It is a remnant of a year of loneliness and swallowed sobs; a year of learning to live with the absence of one parent and the metamorphosis of the other. A year of eating alone at the kitchen table with nothing for company but the crunch or squelch of whatever you are chewing. To this day, when Mummy is greatly agitated, she tugs at the skin inside of her elbow, ripping at it absently with her nails.

My brother turned nine the year Thatcher was thrown out and replaced by the wan, frowny-browed, John Major.

There was a general unease in England, and for some reason the tension manifested itself, at least in the South Asian community through an embracement of religion. For us, it was a clear victory between my amiably doubtful, agnostic mother, and my staunchly Muslim father. Following the example set by others of his family and friends, Baba engaged the services of a maulvi to instruct us in the basics of the Arabic language and the Islamic pillars. We were permitted to hire out the college chapel for our studies, and in my memory, that year is a sleepy-eyed haze of dawn prayers followed by gentle Koran recitations, the musty attar smell of the prayer mats and the gentle, awkward English of our French Arabic teacher.

My brother, errant and unscholarly, would spend much of his morning on 'toilet leave', kicking stones by himself out on the street. It was on one of these jaunts, that he was approached by a man wearing a tweed jacket with leather elbow patches. As my brother watched him, the man unzipped his own trousers, and did something which left my brother speechless and traumatised. Although the man had not touched him, my brother urinated in bed until the age of twelve. And our gentle Arabic teacher was dismissed amidst a cloud of suspicion. The man with the tweed jacket on the other hand is still out there somewhere, frightening the sensibilities of other nine-year old children.

I cannot recall how my teacher was embroiled in this incident. But whether it was by his lie or by his silence, my brother felt he had sent an innocent man to the gallows of eternal unemployability and disrepute, and he carried this guilt around like a long dead conjoined twin down.

A boy that had hitherto been a socialite, a charmer, became a friendless recluse. Where once you would have expected to find him in the playground leading a group of boys on a rampage, you found him now behind a shed, or perched up on the cycle racks, reading any fiction he could get his hands on. And at home, I filled his silences - whether on the kitchen table, in the living room, in the garden. Where once my brother's jovial remarks would have been dispensed with his cheeky grin and met with the grudging laughter of my doting parents, now there was my shrill voice telling tall school girl tales, hoping to entice a laugh. I tried so hard to replace the part of our brother we had lost that year, but that part of him, it turned out, was irretrievable.

We were sharing a desert on our third date, when I first told Salman about my family's Curse of the Nine's, and his chuckle turned almost fatal when a blueberry went the wrong way. The restaurant manager came to the rescue with a forceful Heimlich manoeuvre. As Salman wheezily sipped iced water afterwards, red splotches on his Kashmiri pale skin, I warned him, seriously, that he mustn't laugh in the face of curses like that. He began to laugh again, as I watched on, worried he would choke again, but more worried that he was taunting the curse with his disbelief.

On our wedding day, he shared this part of our early history with the wedding party, adding amidst the audience's teetering, that he loved me so much, he was marrying me in-spite of this tendency to lunacy. I laughed along with everyone that evening, and felt silly when Baba asked me, perplexed, how long I had harboured such a delusion. That night, the idea of the curse retreated as bad things of the past often do, under layers and layers of happy distractions: Baba dancing to the Bee Gees with my crazy Great Aunt; Mummy and my brother sipping gingerly from a little hip flask when they thought my muslim grandparents were not looking, the alcohol building a happy halo of giggles around them; Salman refusing to let go of my hand even once, squeezing my fingers tenderly every now and then. I was blind-sided by those moments and it carried me through the next few years, with barely a thought to the darkness that lurked in me.

The night I held my daughter for the first time, her shock of breathtakingly ebony hair matted against that tender white scalp, I was suddenly overwhelmed by my responsibility for her. There, under the glare of those white hospital halogens, with this bundle of new of bones wrapped in new skin squirming on my chest, a certain murky panic folded itself around me. And those ancient fears resurfaced.

All my loved ones and I had lived through our nines, but the new entry and the most important of them all had yet to live through her's.

Maya is the sort of child, and I do understand that all parents feel this way, but really Maya is the sort of child that everyone is compelled to love. With the sheer force she puts into her greetings and her embraces and her smiles, and the full-throttle nature of her curiosity and excitement, she is the receptacle for all of our loving. She is a magnetic force field and we, her minions, are like mercury drawn in her direction.

As she headed toward nine, my fear grew with her, and it was a fear that didn't care about ridicule. I began to bring it up with Salman, who continued to treat it like some form of insanity, at first with humour, then with some irritation, and then, finally with some serious concern. He asked me to look at it rationally. I refused to. Some things, like God, can't be rationalised. He set up an appointment with a counsellor, and I refused to attend. He enlisted Mummy and Baba, who came over and sat at the kitchen table and tried to coax me out of 'this lunacy'. They left looking dismayed, and a little worried. Salman's fingers tousled my hair less, his gaze left me too soon during conversation, and I felt my grasp on everything begin to feel limp.

Then, one night we caught the end of The Sixth Sense, a much-loved movie, and Salman wondered if I had been looking at the curse all wrong. Like Bruce Willis in the movie, I was too wrapped up in my own need to believe something to think rationally about what had been happening. It was all about perspective. These were Salman's words. Trust a lawyer to make it all about semantics. Why, asked Salman, could I not think of all the good the curse had done? If Baba had not been sent to England, he would not have met Mummy, I would not be here, Maya would not be Maya. Mummy was, in the long-run, better off after the divorce. Better divorced parents than unhappy parents. My period was sort of a funny story in hindsight wasn't it? Glancing at my outraged expression, he concluded it was not, but at least its early appearance made me prepare Maya for her period when she was eight - eight! He added that he couldn't think of a good ending for my brother's experience, but I could ask him that myself.

So, over coffee in the Soho flat my brother lives in, I do ask him.

He looked a little surprised. Like I had asked him to spill his steaming cup of tea onto his fingers. It wasn't a fun conversation. In the intervening decade since it happened, we had not discussed the man with the tweed jacket. I suppose it might have been a tad insensitive of me to bring it up at all. It didn't help matters that I bought it up as a catastrophe that had happened to us but of course it had not happened to us. It had happened to him. As he retorted quite angrily, the curse had its favourites. I got off lightly enough. He wished he had got off with a bit of blood smeared on his underwear. I swallowed my indignation, a little afraid of his fury.

'What about Mr Abdurahman?' I had forgotten our Arabic teacher's name and it surprised me that my brother remembered. But how could he forget? 'Where does he fit into this whole family curse conspiracy theory of yours?' I scavenged for some reply in the icy silence but found none.

My brother pushed his chair back and poured the remainder of his still steaming tea into the sink.

'This whole thing - I know we indulged you because it was funny - but you're starting to take it to another level. There is no curse.' He stood facing me, arms crossed, back pushed against the sink. 'There's NO curse - shit just happens in life.'

I hated myself at that moment. I was staring out at myself from my brother's piercing gaze: staring at a ridiculously privileged, pathetically molly-cuddled younger sibling who was crying for attention. I hated me.

Suddenly my brother was hugging me in my chair. Through the Judas tears that brimmed my eyelids, I saw his softened expression, and hugged him back.

'I suppose,' he said shaking my arm with a consoling smile, 'there's a silver lining most of the time! My stories wouldn't have been quite the same without a filthy pervert in them!' We both laughed, and our laughter rolled around the little kitchen, hollow and tinged with shadows.

I want to make sure as Maya nears her ninth year that she is safe. No amount of talking and sharing stories and looking at different perspectives has made me feel safe, but I need her to be safe.

There will be no birthday party this year. No boxed gifts. I locked away her bike and her scooter in the shed, and I asked her school for extended leave to take her away on the week of her birthday. It would be just the two of us holed up in Cornwall, away from London traffic, and harmful urbanites. Just the friendly estuary and the benign clouds and a trunkful of books and our imagination and us. Salman concealed his irritation and let us go, promising Maya a special belated birthday dinner upon our return. I ignored the frostiness of the kiss we parted with, because, frankly, nothing was as important as keeping Maya safe.

Maya and I spent the last few days eating grilled fish for supper and toasting marshmallows with iron tongs. We read so many Enid Blyton books that we expected the chairs we sat in to fly away with us in them. Salman skyped with us every evening, and was satisfied with the contentment we emitted through the screen as we described our trampolineing competition and our races down to the pier. He held my gaze longer at the end of our calls, even mouthed 'I miss you' on the last couple of nights. I began to feel safe. I began to feel the curse retreat into the corner by the light that we threw on it. Until it came screeching out from the shadows and hurled Maya onto the black tarmac in the hotel car park.

§

Here it is, the worst curse of all the nines. Maya, lying still in my arms, voices around us unpenetrating, because we are in our bubble of mother and baby, skin to skin. Cheek to cold cheek. My fingers entangled in Maya's fingers, still dimpled from infanthood. Perhaps I could breath for her as I had when she was in my stomach. I press my lips to her cold mouth and I breathe, and I breathe and I breathe, and I pray and I pray and I pray.

The ambulance has arrived. Someone puts something

around me and it falls to the floor. I watch as they put Maya on the stretcher, and I wait for the sheet to cover her face.

They do not do this. They do not place a sheet over her face, like in the movies, a symbol of the word I am afraid to use. They put a mask around her face. But mask is okay; sheet is not okay.

I begin to cry. My tears are as afraid of hope as I was once afraid of the curse.

Someone asks if I would like to ride with Maya. What stupidity. I do not answer the stupid person's stupid question. I am led crying, into the space of wires and machines, and I watch Maya.

As I cry I balloon with hysteria and rage. I curse the curse for robbing my Baba's childhood, for taking away my brother's naivety, for bringing destruction to Mummy's home. Suddenly there is no room for fear because every inch of me is consumed with electric rage.

The van begins to move and machines are switched on. I rage and rage until I am spent, and my tears are spent. I am barely breathing, and I am willing my half breaths to go to Maya.

And, despite the curse, they do. She breathes.

As we are driven to the hospital, the two of us, we breathe.

Runaway

Rosie Dastgir

The taxi driver at the airport seemed friendly at first, neither old nor young, but it was hard for Ali to tell. His thickly dyed hair was flat mahogany, and a few tell-tale silver chest hairs peeped through his open necked shirt, but he had a youthful spring to his gait as he made his way across the airport car park. His kind smile made Ali's eyes brim. Perhaps the man would help him.

'Take your time,' said the driver, handing Ali a handkerchief from his trouser pocket, and waiting patiently as he wiped his face. 'There, that's better. What's your name?'

'Ali, sir.'

'So, Ali, tell me what is wrong, a boy of your age shouldn't be crying like this …. how old are you?'

'Four - thirteen,' Ali admitted.

'I thought you seemed older!' the driver exclaimed, a twinkle in his eye. Ali felt a warm gush of confidence, and unburdened himself to the man without a second thought. How he had run away from the madrassa over a hundred miles from here, and how he'd wanted to escape to England. His parents were supposed to come and collect him; they had promised, time and again, but they had never come. They'd forgotten him, he said, left him imprisoned in that place. The driver tutted and sighed in sympathy - that was his forte– and when the boy had finished his tale, he asked him where he and his family lived. Ali trotted out the name of the village, and the driver guessed it was a scant two hour's drive away.

'Let me take you home,' he offered.

Ali hesitated, and shook his head.

'You want a free ride, don't you?' the driver pressed.

Ali bit his lip, and looked down. The man's smile faded.

'Why not?'

'I can't go home,' he wept. 'They'll never forgive me - my father will be so angry.'

The driver wondered what to do, and whether there was another side to his story.

'I would take you to back to my house, but it's difficult today,' he explained, thinking that his wife would not approve. They had no children of their own, and she was reluctant to involve herself with other people's.

'But you can't stay here for the night. It's not really safe in the airport. Come,' he said, opening the car door. The back seat shone in the heat, soft and inviting, and Ali got inside. He was exhausted.

The moment the door slammed, he regretted it. The hot taxi trapped the smell of sweaty bodies and rancid breath, a greasiness that made him gag. The gnawed remains of somebody's lunch lay trodden beneath his feet in an oily slick, and empty plastic bottles covered the floor. He thought of the huge aeroplane, swollen with lucky passengers, soaring overhead without him, and grieved for the life he'd never have.

He had planned to stowaway, he told the driver as they sped along, after planning his escape with another boy, who'd been just as miserable. Yet he'd lost his nerve at the last minute, crouched on the runway, deafened by the roar of the engines. He hadn't expected the noise to be so terrifying. His friend went ahead with it, but he couldn't. The taxi driver listened to this development in the story, privately drawing his own conclusions. Hoping to fly free passage to England this boy! Threatening life and limb and security of other innocent passengers also! It occurred to the man that he'd be richly rewarded for turning him in, if not in this world (almost certainly not), then surely in the next.

It was nearly sunset by the time they pulled up outside a police station on the outskirts of the city.

'Is this where you live, sir?' Ali asked.

The driver smiled. 'No, no. Just wait here, OK? I'll be right back,' he said, and went inside the dilapidated building. It was a shoddy example of Moghul-style architecture, hastily thrown up by the British, with scant attention to the foundations, so that now it appeared to be sinking, its crenellations stained and crumbling, like rotten teeth. Deep fissures mapped the mildewed walls. A wrought iron railing, blistered brown with rust, clung to the verandah's edge for dear life. Ali's fear jellied his bowels, a sensation he had experienced once before when he fell ill travelling on a bus with his parents. He fended off the memory. Too late. A fearsome looseness took hold, threatening to eject his soupy insides right there in the taxi. He lay down on the seat, inhaling its comforting scent in a bid to ease the churning sensation, while he waited for the taxi driver to return. The noise of the door opening made him jump.

'Everything will be fine, Ali, OK?' declared the man cheerfully. 'The police will help you, you can stay here, till your parents come. Just go inside, the officer on duty is waiting.'

Ali's insides roiled, but he said nothing, and did as he was told. He watched as the car bumped over a pothole, and disappeared into the distance.

The station officer was reed thin and prone to gobbing. He scratched his scalp, probed his crotch, his nose and armpits with a blunt pencil, before using it to write down Ali's details and indicating to him to sit upon the floor. Ali obeyed warily. The floor stank, stained with the viscous products of someone's distress.

Time passed. Ali dropped off.

He awoke with a jolt to find himself being dragged into a dimly lit room with the furious policeman screeching in a high pitched voice, white dots of spit flying from his mouth.

'Please, sir, please call my father,' Ali begged the policeman. 'I've done nothing wrong!'

The policeman raised a hand the size of a dinner plate, and slapped him about the head. Pain ricocheted around the walls of his skull like a thwacked squash ball, and he felt his tears betray him for a second time that day. It was far worse than anything he'd ever suffered from the masters at the madrassa, who beat you with sticks when your concentration lapsed. The policeman told him quietly that they would send for his parents only after he had answered questions and explained what he was doing at the airport. Whom he was in league with. The name of the trafficker, the boss man, the gang leader, whoever was behind it, making all the money. While Ali struggled to regain his bearings, the policeman explained that if he did not confess, he would never see his family again. Did he want to see his mother again? Did he want to see her face? Smell her skin? Taste her cooking? Quaking with fear, he nodded that he did.

It was simple. Beautifully so. Confess: go home to your family. Don't confess: well, it was anybody's guess where a boy like him might end up.

Later that evening, as the driver tucked into the tasty supper his wife had cooked for him, he was pricked with remorse about his decision to leave this boy at the police station. When he confided to her what he'd done, she was aghast. No good would come of such a thing, she warned, turning in a boy like that, even if he was part of a criminal gang. The man shrank from his wife's searing disapproval, which penetrated his bones. Unable to sleep that night, he rose at dawn with the intention of tracking down the boy's father, a bricklayer, via the post office in the district where the family lived. He left word with the postmaster about Ali's whereabouts, who promised to pass on the information that afternoon, when Ali's father was due to come and collect some letters he had received. When the man arrived later, the postmaster was so intent on passing on the dreadful news about his son, that he forgot to give him his post. Ali's father was bewildered, but thanked the man gratefully, and took a bus to the outskirts of town, where he found the police station without difficulty.

By the time he arrived at the front desk, he was breathless with asthma, his face and clothes dusty after working since dawn at the building site. A white plastic fan, clogged with mouse-grey gunk, churned the fetid air uselessly. He coughed wheezily, in the hope of gaining attention. But the duty officer took his time making eye contact, for he'd acquired a kind of brutal slowness on the job that served him well.

'Salaam Aleikum,' Ali's father began, when the cough made no impact.

The duty officer did not respond, studying the screen before him.

The brick layer cleared his throat. 'I've learnt that my son, Ali, is here - I have come to collect him. We're struggling, sir, and he was in school a hundred miles away but he ran away ... I am so sorry for the trouble he has caused, he was disobedient in this respect but that is all, no crime committed, please, sir, you know how it is, he's just a boy, he's done nothing wrong. I'm very sorry. Let me at least see him. He is my son.'

The officer peered at him. Another miserable specimen of his countrymen, all of whom delivered the same old routine, performed their bit parts as the poor and downtrodden. Was the boy innocent? Was the father as wretched as he appeared? God alone knew.

'He's not here,' the officer said. 'Your son. There's no record. Who told you he's here?'

'A taxi driver left word for me that he'd picked him up and dropped him here. My son's name is Ali. He's thirteen years old. Have you seen him, sir?'

'And what if I have?'

'Then please help me. My family is all I have in this world,' the man went on. 'I want to bring my boy home.'

'If this boy's your son - and you'll need proof - then you should bring RS 20,000 surety to release him.'

'I don't have this kind of money, sir. How can I do this?'

The officer sighed. 'Then we can't release him.' He was shooing the bricklayer out of the door, when the man said:

'I have a motorcycle.'

The mention of a motorbike made the officer perk up. There wasn't much else going on, to be honest, and he'd go check and see whom he could find.

He tried three interrogation rooms before he located the thin policeman with Ali. The boy was balled up in the corner, panting like a small animal in a trap.

'Are we done with him?' the officer enquired, under his breath. 'The father's come looking.'

The policeman was infuriated at the thought of being deprived of the evening's entertainment. 'Tell him to come back tomorrow,' he muttered.

'OK, baba, so come back tomorrow with the bike and we'll see then,' the duty officer told Ali's father.

'He is here, you say?'

'What did I just say? *Come back tomorrow.* With surety, OK? What kind of motorcycle is it you have?'

'A Honda,' the brick layer replied, trusting his cousin would oblige if he begged him. 'Four years old.'

'Is mileage low?'

'Yes, it is. Please, sir, can I see him?'

'Against regulations. He's with someone now, answering our questions. It's procedure.'

'Thank you, sir, thank you, may Allah bless you.'

The duty officer, who was not a believer, ignored this. He wiped his nose, and resumed work on a thick pile of papers which would never be properly filed. If there were any awkward inquiries ... well, things do go astray, and the bottle of liquid whiteout is a policeman's best friend.

Ali's father stepped outside into the shrill whiteness of

midday. Heat reared up from the scorching brick courtyard and dogged his steps as he trudged towards the gate, spectated by a straggle of guards whose boredom he relieved by tripping over an uneven paving stone. A snigger rippled though their ranks, and one or two adjusted their weapons. His heart thumped so loudly he was afraid they might hear and apprehend him, or worse. But nobody could be bothered. He wasn't important enough, luckily for him. Still, they were holding his son within their walls. The thought propelled him swiftly home.

The following day, he returned to the police station on his cousin's motorcycle, fearlessly slaloming in and out of SUVs and trucks and motorbikes laden with families, only to find that when he presented himself, along with a hastily procured birth certificate, the station officer told him he could not have his son. Not for a motorcycle, Honda or anything else, and not for cash either.

He couldn't have him because he wasn't there, according to the thin policeman, who was in charge that day.

A hot prickling sensation rushed through the father's veins.

'Then where is he, sir?' he asked.

'We were satisfied of his innocence, and the boy was free to go,' the policeman said, his eyes blank. 'We told him you would come and collect him. He didn't believe us. He ran off, that's it.'

The father staggered with the weight of the news.

'But where did he go? He's penniless, just a boy.'

The policeman shrugged. 'The taxi driver who brought him here said he found him at the airport. Maybe he went back there. He was nothing but a runaway.'

**

In the aftermath of Ali's disappearance, the father's work as a bricklayer dried up. The foreman on the building site gave him several chances – he was a good labourer, one of the best – but Ali's father was broken. He did not rise from his bed till noon, leaving the plates of food his wife prepared for him untouched. By night, he kept a vigil, lying awake fretting about his son's uncertain fate. By day, he moped, disconsolate with not knowing. His wife took it upon herself to pray at the saint's shrine, encouraging her husband to do the same, but he had lost faith in everything, human or divine. He returned repeatedly to the airport, scouring it for signs of his boy's whereabouts. One day he quizzed a pair of cleaners who felt sure they had spotted him. Their report gave him purpose and direction, and a sense of hope bloomed within him for a while. And when that sighting came to nothing, he scoured the car park for clues, attracting curious looks from security guards. He pestered the police and the security officers, the airline staff pressed by the hoards behind their desks. He accosted any passers-by who looked like they might remember something. Yet he grew no closer to finding his boy. The more he searched, the more infinite the landscape grew, his son a mere speck in the churning mass of people on this earth. Not a day passed when he didn't rue his decision to send him to that wretched school to his ease his family's burden.

One afternoon, the taxi driver who had picked up Ali noticed him questioning a fellow driver, and idly wondered what he was doing. He was about to intervene and offer assistance, but thought better of it. It was the hottest day of the year, and he had precious little energy for confrontations.

A few weeks later, a letter came from the school, expressing regret about Ali's disappearance. It was followed by a tattered package of his belongings. The father delegated the unwrapping of it to the mother. Within the folds of paper, amongst some threadbare shirts and a pair of flip flops worn smooth with use, she found a collection of things she'd sent him: a compass, some leather trinkets, a handful of sweets, a half empty pickle jar. Without a word, they both understood that Ali had taken matters into his own hands. He was surely alive, they decided, having managed to run away after all, as the policeman claimed. As time went by, they allowed this version of their son's life to take root and grow, like a sapling, flourishing out of sight. They paid occasional visits to the post office, just in case he sent news. The mother washed his flip flops and set them out to dry in the sun, ready to receive his footprint once more. The father wrapped up the rest of the boy's things and put them in a tin trunk stowed under their bed, certain that one day he would return. Perhaps from England.

The Baby

Huma Qureshi

He has a name, thoughtfully chosen from a carefully curated shortlist they spent almost a year compiling, but she still calls him the baby.

Her husband phones and asks her for updates while he is at work. 'The baby is smiling,' she says. 'The baby needs a change.'

Sometimes she looks down at her lap while she is on the phone to her husband, while the baby kicks out at her or stares at her from his mat on the floor, and she does not know what else to say.

Today, the baby is crying.

'He won't stop,' she says.

'Have you tried feeding him?'

She does not answer, for she thinks surely it must be obvious that would be the first thing she might have tried.

Her husband suggests rocking the baby, bouncing him, feeding him again.

She is exhausted otherwise she would explain, she would snap, perhaps, that she has already tried doing each of those things, several times. But she is tired, so she says nothing at all.

Her husband says he cannot hear properly because the

baby is crying too loud. She continues to hold the handset of her mobile phone to her ear with her free hand, until she realises that he has already hung up.

***

They had planned it, the pregnancy. They had always agreed they would start trying this year. Last year was about her promotion, his securing financing for a particular business deal. But this year was about the baby. That is what they had always said.

But Rakhi had thought it might take months, years even. That is what all her friends had told her. She did not think it would happen so quickly. Certainly not as fast as it did.

She conceived on New Year's Eve. The end of one year, the start of the next. That night, they had dinner with neighbouring friends in north London, three other sets of couples seated around a large wooden table on fashionably scratched chairs. She had worn an expensive velvet dress, chandelier earrings, high heels. They ate veal parmigiana, drank vintage wine and then tumbled late, loudly, into their white stucco townhouse.

As they entered, Rakhi left her heels in the hallway and dropped her winter coat on the floor. She scattered her scarf across the bed, stepped out of her expensive dress and let it fall into a heavy, luxurious heap, collapsing like a theatre curtain at the end of a show. Simon, who even inebriated had little patience with Rakhi's dishevelled habits, followed her, picking up the pieces of the trail she had left behind.

Rakhi was ready for bed, but Simon came in with red wine and glasses, joking that she might not be able to drink it much more. It would not happen so fast, Rakhi warned him. But still, he toasted to the year ahead.

'This time next year, there might be three of us,' Simon whispered.

'Perhaps,' Rakhi said. 'Perhaps.'

Several weeks later, Rakhi sat at her desk during her lunch hour, responding to a message from friends inviting them over to eat. She turned the pages of her diary to check they were free on the day they had suggested, penciling it in on the page. She was about to confirm when she realised, the thin printed pages of her diary fluttering through her fingertips, that she was significantly overdue.

She did not feel a surge of excitement at the possibility of pregnancy, as the other women she met later in her antenatal class described. Instead, she sat for a few minutes, feeling her cheeks turn first cold then flushed with feverish panic. She covered her face with her hands, grateful for the large silver computer screen which sheltered her from her colleagues. But then her desk phone rang abruptly, a message for her from reception announcing a client's arrival for their meeting that afternoon, and she forced the possibility entirely out of her mind.

Rakhi waited three weeks before she took a test. She did not tell Simon. She could not sleep. On the nights when Simon kissed her shoulder and asked her if it might be time to try again, she nudged him aside, said they had plenty of time.

She had no idea, really, why she felt like this. They had planned for this. They had decided it would be this year. It was always what they had said they would do.

Eventually she bought a home pregnancy test on her way back from work. She scanned it quickly at the self-checkout in the high street chemist, stuffing it into her bag. Even though her heart paced wildly when she saw the two lines affirmatively appear, she smiled as she held it out for Simon to see. She turned to him, trembling into his chest.

'Yes darling, I'm so happy too,' she quietly said.

***

The baby is still crying. Rakhi does not know what to do with him. She puts him on the floor, laying him down on his garish, cushioned play mat. She turns away from him because she does not know what else to do.

The baby screams, high pitched and relentless, as if the world is collapsing in on his tiny, grasping lungs.

Rakhi pretends she cannot hear him and goes to make herself a cup of tea. She turns the washing machine on. She wipes down the kitchen counter. She does anything, really, that she can in the few minutes her hands are free.

Rakhi walks back into the living room. She tries not to look in the baby's direction but she can feel his shiny, liquid eyes watching her.

'Stop looking at me.'

She turns around.

The baby stares at her, his legs twitching this way and that.

'What do you want? Why are you looking at me?' she asks sharply.

The baby whimpers sadly like his miniature heart has cracked, as if he recognises that his mother's tone is not kind. Rakhi sits down on the sofa, her mug of tea in her hand. She exhales. She sets the mug down on the side table and rubs her forehead with her tremoring hands. She closes her eyes. She sits like this in silence while the baby cries.

Eventually she looks up, stares at the wall, shakes her head out of the stupor she is so often in. 'He's just a baby, he's just a baby, he's just a baby,' she recites, blinking away the saltiness she feels in her eyes before sliding down to the floor to sit by his side. She kneels awkwardly to pick him up and then begins to rock him from side to side.

In the beginning the baby's throaty cries made Rakhi panic. Often she felt like shaking him, just to make him stop. She did not know to hold him close, to rub his unfurling back. She did not know to stroke his cheek with her fingertip, to settle him with the warmth of her flesh, the smell of her skin, the hot hum of her breath. She did not know to whisper soft, sweet love notes close to his tiny ear. None of this came to her like magic.

Rakhi only knows to rock the baby and bounce him because that is what everyone else tells her she should do. She feels clumsy and self-conscious when she picks him up, because she cannot shake the feeling that she is doing it wrong.

Sometimes (and Simon does not know this, because he never sees) when the baby's cries reach a shrillness that might splinter her skull, Rakhi carries the baby upstairs and puts him down in his cot. She closes the door and leaves him there and does not look behind her as she walks down the stairs and slumps on the sofa, staring at the wall, wiping the corners of her sore eyes.

***

Simon took time off for Rakhi's pregnancy scans. He rearranged meetings on the days she had midwife appointments so he could go with her and hold her hand, even though Rakhi told him repeatedly that the check ups were routine, that there was no need for him to be there at all.

But he insisted. He met her at Liverpool Street and helped her on to the tube, resting his hand in the small of her back. He always asked, if the seats were taken, if Rakhi could sit down.

'She's pregnant, you see.'

'No, honestly, I'm fine.'

'Darling, you'll get tired. Sit.'

And so Rakhi would sit, apologetically.

Simon was anxious about everything. He clenched Rakhi's hand every time her blood was taken, every time her urine was tested with a dipstick.

The day they found out the baby was a boy, Simon cried. The sonographer had left them alone for a moment. Rakhi was struggling to wipe the cold, thick gel off her bulging stomach with thick wads of scratchy tissue paper, trying hard not to get it on her dry-clean only black top.

'Darling,' Simon said, stilling her hands with his. 'A boy!'

Rakhi smiled at him. She kissed him back. But she was propped up uncomfortably on her elbows and the cold plastic cover of the examination couch was sticking to her skin and all she wanted to do was to get off the tacky sheet. Simon kept his hands on top of hers and as he squeezed, Rakhi noticed the glutinous gel had already smeared along the hem of her blouse.

On the way out of the hospital, Simon phoned his parents, his brother and sister, his best friend. He described to each of them how he felt, the unbelievable miracle of seeing his baby, his son, swoop and swim on the sonographer's machine. He had requested extra photographs, he would send one to them all.

'Yes, Rakhi's fine. She's doing so, so well,' he said, beaming at her in the taxi on the way to the restaurant that Simon had booked as a post-scan surprise.

Rakhi listened to Simon on the phone, holding his hand, picking at the filmy residue of white gel which trailed along the edge of her top. She looked at Simon sideways and wondered if he was exaggerating for effect. She thought he probably was. She thought that was typically Simon. She did not feel any of what he was describing, and the baby was inside her after all.

Rakhi said she would call her family and her friends later.

But in the end, she sent them an email with 'The baby' typed in the subject line. She did not write much, just one or two lines, and attached a photograph of the scan for them to see so that they could draw the conclusion of the baby's sex themselves.

'Don't you want to talk to them?' Simon asked. 'Don't you want to tell them yourself?'

'It will be more of a surprise this way,' Rakhi said. 'It will build up the suspense. They will see it's a boy.'

But, really, Rakhi did not want to talk to anyone at all.

***

Simon keeps looking up things for Rakhi to do during the day, as if she is on holiday.

He puts together lists of baby-friendly places she can visit in London, places she can walk to so she doesn't have to catch the tube. He searches on the internet while he is at work for local mother and baby groups. He insists she stay in touch with the new mums they met through their antenatal classes, keeps telling her to invite them over. He looks for parks with play areas, even though the baby is only three months old.

Simon is delighted, because he has discovered a baby singalong that takes place in a local coffee shop on Upper Street, a short walk away. He tells her there is a session in the morning and urges Rakhi to go. He spends all evening talking about it over their takeaway dinner.

'I don't like singing,' Rakhi says. 'And the baby won't

understand, anyway. So, there's no point.' Rakhi thinks it is stupid. A singalong, for babies who cannot even speak.

But Simon insists. He says it will be good for her to leave the house. He says he does not understand why she is being so negative, why she will not even consider trying it out.

'Call one of the antenatal class girls, go with them,' he says. And when she does not respond: 'You're lucky you get to spend all this time with him. I'd swap places with you in a second.'

'Really?' Rakhi says, throwing a tea towel on the floor. 'You would, would you?'

The baby wakes up disturbed and starts crying. Rakhi shakes her head, wordlessly. Simon touches her arm, tells her he will go and check on the baby instead. 'Makes a change,' Rakhi says, furiously.

Simon sleeps in the guest room on the third floor. It was decided, before the baby was born, that Simon would need to sleep in order to be able to function at work. But there is nothing Rakhi hates more than sharing her room with the baby. At night, she stares at the bedroom ceiling, hearing the guest bed creak as Simon settles in for a restful sleep. She clenches her jaw, not sure who she resents more, Simon or the baby.

Tonight, after a day of crying, the baby is particularly unsettled. He wakes up every hour, demanding tedious, long breastfeeds. Each time the baby cries, Rakhi covers her head with her pillow. At one point, she locks herself in the ensuite, waiting for Simon to wake up and realise how exhausted she is. But he never comes.

'He's just a baby, he's just a baby, he's just a baby,' Rakhi recites to herself, her forearms leaning on the cold porcelain sink. She splashes water on her face and then returns to the baby, picks him up and latches him on to her, pushing her head back against the pillows she props herself up with. She falls asleep as she breastfeeds him, and in the morning when Simon comes in for a fresh shirt from the wardrobe, he is horrified to see she did not put the baby back in his cot.

'It's dangerous to keep him in bed, darling,' he says. 'I know you are tired, but you must try to be careful.'

Rakhi stares at Simon in disbelief. Then she shakes her head.

'What?' asks Simon. 'Nothing,' she says. She asks him, flatly, to take the baby so she can brush her teeth.

Before he goes to work, Simon assembles the pushchair and sets it by the front door so that Rakhi does not need to put it together by herself. 'The singalong starts at ten,' he says.

Rakhi ignores him as he kisses first her forehead, then the baby's, before he leaves.

***

Before the baby was born, they signed up to weekly antenatal classes. All summer, they spent their Tuesday nights squashed up in the living room of a former midwife, now an antenatal and breastfeeding expert, along with six other couples who lived nearby. The men came in work suits, loosening their collars. The women wore smart office skirts, sculpted over their protruding pregnant stomachs. At the first meeting, they talked about the novelty of having left work on time to make it to the class.

Rakhi did not want to go. It was expensive and, she said to Simon, she did not think they would learn much about having a baby sat in someone else's front room.

'It's not about that,' said Simon. 'It's about making new friends with people who are having babies at the same time.'

The couples all worked in finance and law, business and marketing. Because of this, Simon reassured Rakhi that they would find things in common, be compatible as friends. Outside of the classes, the women talked about their midwife appointments, the size of their bumps, hospital reviews they had read online as if they were browsing hotels.

Sometimes, they met at The Albion on Sundays for drinks. The men stood by the bar, the women, their flip-flopped feet swollen from the heat, sat on benches with scatter cushions tucked into the small of their aching backs.

'All we talk about is babies,' said Rakhi, after one afternoon in which the women discussed brands of nappies and the sizing of baby sleep suits.

'What did you expect?' asked Simon, who rather enjoyed spending his time with the boys, as he called them.

During their classes and their get-togethers, Rakhi watched these women, the way their hands absent-mindedly caressed their stomachs. She wondered whether any of them felt the panic she did. She wondered if they sometimes stared at themselves in the mirror, fraught with sickening fear, the way she did every night.

***

It is already after ten by the time Rakhi and the baby are ready to leave, wrapped up in layers to keep warm. She knows it is too late. The singalong only lasts forty minutes and they have missed nearly half of it.

'It's your fault,' she says to the baby. 'You made us late.'

The baby smiles at her, gumless and milky.

Rakhi does not know what to do, but she supposes she might as well walk some place, now that she has completed the task of getting herself and the baby dressed and out of the house.

She walks without thinking, up and down the parallel streets of Barnsbury where they live. She enters a quiet, large garden square the size of a swimming pool, surrounded by a circle of white stucco houses similar to their own. She does a lap, and then sits on a cold, wrought iron bench. The baby is asleep.

Rakhi stands up, and takes a few footsteps away from the pram, considering how far she might go before the baby wakes up. He does not stir. She tests him. She sets herself a distance. First she walks to a tree, just a few metres away. She comes back; the baby does not stir. Then she walks to the next bench and back. Still, he does not stir. She ventures further, emboldened by her daring. She touches the edge of the square, then the next bench after that. She does not walk back to check, then, because she knows she will hear the baby if he cries.

She walks, without the tedious attachment of the pram, and she does not think of anything, feeling only the stretch in her legs which have spent the last three months, at the very least, cooped up inside.

She reaches the gate of the square, and it is then that she looks behind her. The rest of the square is still. The only person to have stirred through the leafless trees was a young woman out running, but that was fifteen minutes ago. The pram with its bright yellow shade sits there like a silent beacon, calling.

'I could leave him,' she thinks simply. 'I could just leave him.'

She does not even realise that she is moving further and further away. She feels nothing, entirely.

***

One by one, the couples from their antenatal class announced the arrivals of their new babies. The new, shell-shocked fathers wrote emails and texts, shared anecdotes of being birth partners.

The women sent emails to each other, often in the early hours. They wrote about their tiredness, about problems with latching their babies on to feed. A few mentioned the searing, burning pain that lingered still. But then they wrote about how it was all worth it. About how they would do it, all over again, just to hold their perfect babies in their arms.

As her own due date crept closer, Rakhi reassured herself that she would feel the same, that she too would feel the same overwhelming surge of unconditional love, instantly and unquestionably. That she would fall madly, deeply, uncontrollably in love with her baby, and that all her fear and anxiety would dissipate. That she would be maternal. That it would be magic.

She kept telling herself this, all the while, even when she stood in the shower at nine months pregnant, staring at her stomach as if it was not a part of her at all.

***

Rakhi has been walking for ten minutes. She has not made it very far. She has crossed the road, and is now at the end of a small side path. The square is still behind her. She turns around and she can still make out the pram in the distance, with its bright yellow shade, sheltered under bare branches.

It takes her a moment to register that she is not where she is supposed to be. And then the panic hits her.

She runs, crosses the road and enters the square again through an iron gate. Her heart is pumping. She does not even know how long she has been away, stood on the small side path

'He's just a baby, he's just a baby, he's just a baby,' she recites, breathless by running even this short distance, for it has been so long since she has moved her legs in this way. She is only vaguely aware of the tears that are stinging her face.

She reaches the pram and she swallows for air when she sees the baby, still sleeping, his cheeks pink from the freshness of the winter air. He looks helpless, unaware, cradled beneath the fleece sleeping bag. It hurts Rakhi to swallow, dry clusters of sour tasting vomit blocking her throat.

Rakhi is struggling to breathe. She steadies herself, sitting on the bench, placing one hand on the pram. She looks at the baby. She pushes the heels of her hands into her face, then throws her head back to the sky.

'He's just a baby,' she cries. She cries, until the baby stirs, and they walk home in a silence punctuated only by the baby's milky, creamy gurgles.

***

Rakhi lay helplessly on her back, wires and tubes stabbed into her swollen hands. It was a nineteen-hour labour. She hated every minute of it.

It was traumatic. The baby was in distress. Rakhi's blood pressure plummeted several times, causing crash teams to run in, shout things that Simon did not understand. There was an emergency cesarean and it took longer than necessary for the baby's cry to come. Simon was a wreck. Rakhi was in too much worn-out pain to register most of what was going on.

When eventually the baby was handed to her, grasping for her breast with a wrinkled mouth, Rakhi waited for it to make sense. She waited to fall in love. But all she felt was the fear, again, that she had made the worst mistake of her life.

When they eventually got home after four brutally uncomfortable nights in the hospital, Rakhi did not write to tell the women from her antenatal class all about her experience. She thought she would rather forget.

***

It is May. The living room in their townhouse is flooded with a clear, bright sunlight every morning. When Rakhi puts the baby down to play, he reaches into the light, which makes a triangular pattern on the wooden floor, and he grasps at it, as if it were an object for him to put into his mouth.

After that cold morning, when Rakhi left the baby in the square, she called her health visitor. She told her how she felt. She told her she cried uncontrollably most nights. She told her she was exhausted, that her body hurt almost all the time. She told her that sometimes, she looked at her baby, and she did not understand what he wanted or who he was.

She did not tell her over the phone that she had left the baby alone in the square. But when the health visitor came over, with a concerned face and warm hands that held hers, Rakhi whispered it, confessed it like a sin. For the first time, she opened up to someone about her biggest fear, about not loving the baby at all.

The health visitor was kind. She told Rakhi that bonding could be difficult, that it did not mean the connection would never come. She arranged for Rakhi to see doctors and organised counselling. For the first time, Simon began to see she was struggling. It took him time to realise that motherhood was not parks and coffee mornings. It was not baby singalongs.

But the baby is bigger now. He does more things. Rakhi plays with him, and she is learning his habits. She likes the softness of his hair. She likes to feel his hot breath on her cheek. Sometimes, when Rakhi stands in front of him, barefoot, the baby delights in pulling at her toes. It tickles Rakhi and she laughs. When she does this, the baby turns his head up from his turtle-like position on the floor. With his thick soft fingers splayed over Rakhi's feet, he grins at her, a huge wet pink smile, and then she says his name, and smiles back at him.

Table for Two

Susmita Bhattacharya

The Chinese family across the street are cooking their tea. Into this cold grey evening they let out the smell of garlic and lemongrass. The steam from their kitchen condenses on the window, creating a soft blur of the family chatting, laughing and setting the table.

Their bin flew open one blustery morning, spewing out a burst of the orient onto our bleak street. Green tea packets, golden peanut biscuit wrappings, crumpled red boxes of chrysanthemum tea. Ribbons with bold black calligraphy fluttered in the trees for days.

They look like porcelain dolls, with shiny black hair and alabaster skin. The little girl rides her bike on the path, her small face peeking out through the fur-lined hood. She laughs and chases her cat while pedalling furiously down the road. Her mother calls after her, speaking fast and urgently. She sounds like the blackbird that sings in my backyard. The little girl returns, cuddling the cat and pushing her bicycle up to her doorstep. She then sits on the step, petting her cat and waits until her father drives home from work. He toots his horn and she jumps up and down. The cat stretches its body long on the path, waiting to have its tummy tickled.

Together they go in, where the mum, still in her Boots uniform, grins at them and closes the door.

Evening is my favourite time of day because they are all home for tea. I leave the window open, no matter what the weather, and take in deep breaths. The fragrance of meat and rice remain suspended in the air, enveloping me in a cosy embrace. I don't really know what they eat at home, but I'm sure that it's better than my plastic wrapped cottage pie.

I like to close my eyes and imagine their table. Noodles wound expertly on chopsticks, with lashings of a dark sweet sauce and strips of pork. That's what I watch on telly. Cookery shows. Chinese. Indian. Even British. So why is my korma never so inspiring, or my toad-in-hole so disappointing? Is it because they take two minutes to heat up in the microwave?

I'm not allowed near a fire. I'm not capable, they say. I cannot handle a knife. I may cut myself. I'm not allowed a job anymore. I used to be a postman. I trekked for miles, with bags of letters slung across my shoulders. I attended a creative writing evening course once. I even had a short story in the local magazine. I met a woman there. We wrote poetry together. Made love under the stars. Drank too much wine. And then I began to forget her name. I began leaving the front door open. I began to mix up my mail.

Now the only woman who visits me is my carer. And of late, even she is not a constant. There's a new one every other week. The first one was nice, asked me in a loud voice how I was and never waited for the answer. But always made a cup of tea for me. But now they don't have time for a cuppa, they barely wash me down before they are rushing off to their next client. No hellos or goodbyes. They flit in and out the door, trying to keep up with their heavy schedules. It's not their fault. It's all the governments cuts that done it. Cutting back on carers, might as well shoot us dependents down. Save money all the way that way. Money to build high speed train tracks for very busy and important people. I am not a person for any of them, just a body to be washed. I have a mind that works sometimes, but most of the time it goes on autopilot. I'm very good at sitting by the window. All day. I used to write about my world, a long time ago. Now I just sit, and watch.

And one day, I see a new face at the window opposite.
She's tiny, this old lady, deep wrinkles like sand dunes lining her face. Her eyes, what little I can see of them, are full of happiness. She catches my eye and gives me a grin. She has two yellow teeth but she's not embarrassed to show them off. She must be the girl's grandmother, I think. She waves and turns away.

*

She's outside my window, waving her arms like a madwoman. I shuffle to the door, not looking forward to confront to her. I don't do talking, only watching. I have to bend down to look at her. She's pulling at my hand, talking gibberish. I stumble out and follow her. I'm still in my vest and I smell. I haven't had a wash for some time now. I have refused to let the carer touch my body. I enter their house unsure of what's happening. The old woman takes me out to the garden and points to a tree. The cat is mewling up there. She pushes me towards the tree, her eyes shedding tears down her lined face. I stop to observe her. She looks like a river, thousands of rivulets coursing down her face, slipping down her throat into her bosom. She sniffles and rubs her nose, wipes her hands on her dress and points up to the tree again.

There's a ladder by the shed and we both move it to the tree. I haven't climbed a ladder in years. I feel shaky, tearful. I want to go home, back to my armchair. What if I fall? I don't want to go into a home. Oh no, I don't. I can just about manage myself now. But this old woman will be the end of me. I don't have to climb much. Just three rungs up and I can reach the bloody cat. It's baring its teeth at me, hissing. Cheeky sod. I have the cat down and in the lady's arms. She bows to me. Now I am embarrassed. She leads me in, talking all the time. I nod, as though I know exactly what she's saying.

She sits me down at the table and offers me a drink. It is yellow with flowers floating in it, and it stinks. I press my lips together in a smile and wonder how to get rid of the stuff without offending her. I'm still in my vest and still smelling, so I really need to go home. She nods her head vigorously, showing me her two teeth again and pours some more of it in my cup.

I try to excuse myself. I shouldn't get upset, I keep reminding myself. I'm not very good at being upset. I should go, really. But she's gaping at me, nodding and smiling. I start to breathe faster and faster. I need fresh air. The kitchen's too hot. There are pots bubbling on the stove, releasing enough steam to make me sweat. There are too many things in the room. Tins and tins of food. Blue plastic bags with some kind of leaves spilling out on the dining table. Chopped carcass of a chicken on the cutting board, a steel cleaver gleaming in the kitchen light. Calendars with Chinese numbers and photos untidily tacked on the fridge. Red fringed decorations hanging on the walls. A big paper lantern floating above me. My head is spinning. I don't manage well in clutter. I need white, clean space. I need to go home.

She retreats, as if understanding my problem. I think she's afraid now that I'm standing straight and tall, towering over her miniscule body. When she looks up at me, she folds her hands together and dips her head. She then strokes the cat, nuzzling its ear. She lays it in a basket. There's a cushion in the basket with Hello Kitty printed on it. I push back the vile liquid and shake my head. She watches me and steps back. Slowly, she moves to the gas stove and starts to tend to the cooking pots. She stirs, tastes, and adds something. She chops mushrooms and carrots with a staccato beat, creating matchsticks of vegetable that she chucks into the smoking wok.

I watch her. Her expectations mesmerise me. It's better when she's ignoring me. She adds the chicken to the pot. I like the aroma wafting in the room. Slowly, I walk towards her and inspect the cooking pots. So what do the Chinese cook for their tea?

I learn as I watch. She cooks with a passion that breaks my heart. No one's cooked with love for me as far as I can remember. I lived on baked beans and boiled potatoes as a child. Scraps of meat were the Sunday special. When she finishes, she motions me back to the table. She takes the offending drink away and sets down a place for me. I watch as she ladles food in little bowls. We sit down and eat. My first cooked meal in a very long time. She slurps and licks and chews noisily. I follow enthusiastically. Her cat purrs contentedly in the basket, curls into itself and sleeps.

After the meal, she takes a framed photo of the family and shows it to me. She pokes a bony finger at the woman, who is smiling at the camera. Her eyes are so slanted that they are just slits in her face. Her smile is full of teeth. She's the mother, I can see. I haven't ever seen her so up close before. The old lady strokes the woman's hair in the photo, and I realise that's her daughter. The man, with his thinning hair, isn't grinning as much. He's peering through his glasses, looking like he is wasting time posing. He should be somewhere else. And their little girl, the porcelain doll, well, she is even more of a doll, as a little baby. She kisses the baby and places the photo on the mantelpiece again. She smiles at me. She folds her hands together and nods.

It is time to go. I shuffle along to my house. She follows me out. I know she's going to pick up the little girl from school. I return to my armchair and doze a bit. I wait for the evening soap. I look around my house and smile. I will be more helpful to the lady who comes in to clean. I will have a wash tonight and wear fresh clothes. I look forward to waving to her in the morning during the school run. I realise that today I haven't heard my microwave go 'ping'.

My Brother Vrinder

Palo Stickland

I loved my brother Vrinder, from the very day he was born. I was on the other side of the cotton sheet that split our room in two, when I heard him take his first cry, and I rushed to take a look. I was ten years of age, had been lying, with eyes wide open, on the floor of the shack where I lived with my parents. I watched as the woman from the clinic wrapped him in a shawl before placing him at the side of my mother.

Ma smiled at me. 'Come here. See, this is your brother. You are my Ram, he is your Lakshman. Remember, it's your duty to take care of him.'

Lying down on the mat beside them, I placed my hand over his tiny fingers before answering, 'Yes, Ma. I will do that.'

I knew about the God Ram whose name was also mine. Long years ago, he had been forced into exile with his wife Sita. His younger brother, Lakshman, had refused to remain in the palace without him, living in the jungle for thirteen years, taking a vow of celibacy. Each year, I watched with fascination the enactment of his life in the town square; the exile and the war that began when he rejected the advances of the sister of the ten-headed demon who lived in Sri

Lanka. My brother Vrinder would be like Lakshman, a man of honour. I was not to know that fate decreed a different path for us.

At the time of his birth, I was working as a balloon-seller in the market. Each evening, I hurried home to play with him, while my mother cooked our meal. My father was a driver on the trucks that carried goods across India. On his trips home, he would stay with us for a day, sometimes two, before he was called away again.

I had attended school for three years, could read and write in Hindi, when my mother withdrew me saying, 'That is all the schooling you need. The money you will bring by working will help us, even if it's only a rupee a day.'

I supported my brother; held him when he took his first steps, pronounced words for him when he spoke with a lisp and dried his tears when our mother died.

I had come home one day to find my aunt, my father's sister, in the shack. She sat behind the curtain with my mother whose sobbing was audible to us on the other side. Vrinder and I lay down to sleep. In the night we woke to the sound of her vomiting. Whatever my mother had taken killed her before the morning. At first light, as the smell of wood smoke from morning fires covered the other smells of the shanty town, the men from neighbouring shacks took her body away without ritual or ceremony.

My aunt said, 'I can't help you now, boys. I have a family living in one room in the city. Your father has another woman. Your mother thought he would come for you, if she took poison, but I know he won't. Ram, you must care for your brother now.'

I was fourteen, Vrinder four. He would not speak about what had happened that night; only when I sent him to school did he begin to smile again.

At that time, I had been apprenticed to the local sweetmeat maker. He was a good man who taught me everything he knew, enabling me to open my own shop near the town's level crossing.

It's a busy place, as the trains pass at regular intervals the barriers are lowered. The traffic queue builds up, the waiting public buy sweets, pakoras and samosas from me, cooked with fresh ingredients, as I sit cross-legged at the fryer.

'Hello, Ram.'

It is one of my customers.

'How is the family these days?'

'Everyone is well. Here is my son learning how to run the shop. I'll be able to retire soon.' I laugh at my fourteen year old who knows I am joking. I would not take him from his studies.

'And what of your brother who was studying at college. He went abroad, didn't he?'

'Yes, he is very well. Working in an office, a bank,' I exaggerate but that is expected by my customers. 'He is back home this month, on a visit.'

'He's still single, then? You've given him everything else, now you must find a bride.'

'We're looking for an educated girl.'

'Of course, that's the way it is nowadays. I'll have 400 grams of pakoras, Ram.'

'Coming up,' I smile.

At the end of each day, I am in the habit of locking up the shop before making my way to the beer bar, to exchange a few pleasantries over a drink. Since Vrinder's arrival a week ago I've been waving aside the calls of my friends to join them. I know they understand, as I continue along the main street towards the house where I rent two rooms in a small complex. Three families share a courtyard, toilets and washrooms. We are cramped for space but supportive of each other. Safe accommodation is difficult to find here; we are happy enough. I remember how I took a tiny room in this house so Vrinder and I could leave the shanty town; it was one of the store cupboards in the house, but we managed. When a room with a veranda space for a kitchen became available I took it; I could not have married Shila without a decent place to live. Vrinder was at college when I accepted her father's offer of marriage. The go-between had told me she was very pretty, educated to fifth grade. I smile at the memory. We are a happy, loving couple. She's a good wife, I'd be lost without her. We only have the one son but I know he will do well in life; an intelligent, obedient boy.

I arrive at my house, my son will be at evening tuition; I push the heavy gate, cross the courtyard where the neighbour's little ones play cricket and I lift the curtain of the door to my room. My breath catches in my throat at the scene before me; the nightmare begins...

I stare at the straight cold lines of the railroad; two tracks, one going west, the other east. Moving my head, in slow motion as if it does not belong to my body, I manage to look to my left. Two hundred metres away is the level crossing, the motor-cycles ranged along both sides ready to take off when it opens again. The smell of their exhaust fumes wafts towards me on the slight breeze. Turning my head, in the same dreamlike motion, I look to my right where I can make out that the station platform is not crowded with would-be passengers. That means it's the Delhi express, it will pass through at speed. I return to gazing at the track while people walk on the dirt road behind me, taking no notice of my bowed head, hunched shoulders, my hands clenched in my armpits and the tears in my eyes. How to make sense of what I've seen in that room; my dusty stumbling to the rail track – what use is this life?

I hear the steady rumble of cars and long distance carriers on the national highway which runs parallel to the railway. This is a busy growing town, but it is time for me to leave it, to die now.

A cow, with her calf, stops behind me, I can smell the fresh dung she drops. I cannot move, though I feel a touch on my trouser leg. I have stood so still that a dog has dared to come close. But no, this is no dog, someone is grovelling in the dust beside me, crying, sobbing. It is Shila.

Ah, the love of my life, my queen, it has come to this.

'Get away, you bitch!' It is my voice.

I flash a look of derision and rage at the stooped figure. This can't be the bride I married. She was so beautiful that day; I was the happiest man in India. My brother Vrinder had stood beside me, taking his rightful place; there was singing and dancing, now our lives are in ruins.

Shila sobs. 'Please come home, you are everything to me. I am so sorry. So sorry.'

'Sorry now?' I hear myself say.

'I was stupid. We were carried away. Please do not stand here, a train is coming on this track.'

Someone is running towards me from my right, kneeling on the gravel, grabbing my leg at the knee and shouting. 'Brother, come home. What are you doing? It's not what you think. Please.'

It is Vrinder, I can see his smart foreign shirt; his finely-pressed trousers are picking up dirt from the ground. My heart lifts, my brother has come for me. But it's not easy to take a step away from where I stand, having decided to die.

How can I go back? The fair-skinned foreign-returned rich man. Who could blame Shila for falling for him? My confident little brother, easy with his jokes. Was it only minutes ago that life fell apart? Shila with Vrinder on top of her, kissing, laughing. How stupid of me to walk in on them; then not back away without a fuss. They'd turned, both wet mouths puffed with the pressure and pleasure from kissing; both still open showing white teeth. Shila's pink cheeks, Vrinder's darker face, bright shining eyes, their surprised looks, and the choked cry, mine, as I turned and ran.

Now they are both here; I shake my legs again, to free myself of them.

'I raised you my little brother, paid the agents to send you to a better life, and this is your thanks. You couldn't keep your hands off my pretty wife, you didn't even think of our son, your nephew.' I am blubbering, the tears running down my cheeks.

The smell of stale frying oil, from my clothes, reminds me of my shop and I turn to look in the direction of the level crossing. The rhythm of the approaching train vibrates through the rails. The rumble of its wheels, steel on steel and its pervasive, insistent hooting pierce the air. I watch the blue carriages pass on the far line, will my muscles to rush for the track, but my brother grabs my knee, at the same time as my wife pulls my arm. I stretch forwards pushing her back as the carriages, the people hanging on the doors, others sitting at the windows, go by. No matter, the next train will be on this nearer track. I will wait a little longer, with my thoughts.

My brother, my wife, they will never be forgiven. Our community is everywhere and will ostracise them. They will be given no favours, no place to stay, no place to hide. They will live with strangers but still, people will discover their past and repeat again and again, 'Look, that's Shila and Vrinder who were caught making love by her husband. He killed himself. Shame on them.'

But what of my son? My son whose life will be tainted, as was mine by the whispers in the shanty town, though my mother had done no wrong. I throw my hands to my ears.'

'Look at them, their mother was a whore.'

'You're the son of a whore, Ram.'

I hear myself scream, 'Mother, mother! I did my duty all of my life. I obeyed your command, Mother. Forgive me now.'

On the other side of the two tracks there is a gathering of people shaking their heads. I can sense their words, 'Poor Ram, he's lost his mind.'

My son is there; I see him poised to race across the tracks towards me. I would do anything for my son.

I grip Vrinder's shoulder to ready myself, he senses this and shouts, 'No brother! Please, no!'

We struggle. I pull away, while he pulls me back. I hurl myself forward as the train hurtles along the track with horn blaring as if in expectation of death, of blood on the tracks.

Vrinder clings to me. I push hard, let go as … he loses his balance, trips over the throbbing line and slips under the cruel wheels of the train.

I hear screams, raise myself tall, the carriages pass with their usual rhythmic heartbeats.

My son races into my arms, stepping across the parts of a body that was my brother Vrinder.

'He slipped, Vrinder slipped, I saw it happen,' a voice behind me. I feel relief.

I hear Shila screaming amongst the clamour of other female voices.

'What a tragedy. Take your family home, Ram,' my friend's voice, loud to let all hear. 'We'll deal with the police;

we saw what happened. We'll bring Vrinder, what's left of the poor man. Go home, yarh. You were a good brother. Go.'

He pats me on the back. I nod and turn away.

Don't Tell the Children

Priya Khanchandani

THEY SIT TOGETHER in the living room, she with her nose against the television and he on the easy chair behind, wrapped in a fleece blanket, a furry deerstalker hat on his head with the ear flaps down. Laxman always wears the hat in winter, even when the heating is on full blast, even in bed. The screen flickers, an alarmed woman's face against a red wall at one moment, then the lightning flash of the sky. They are watching Humsafar and Karan has just found out that Rachna is only marrying him for his money. Padma can just about make out the shadows of characters and flashes of light when she watches at an angle up close, but follows intently with her ears.

It is the same most evenings at this time, she sitting inches from the television and he wrapped up on the sofa behind her in their home, a three-bedroom semi wallpapered with two generations worth of memories. They don't answer phone calls and even miss the doorbell when their son occasionally turns up to check on them, as the television is turned up so high it drowns everything else out. It fills their now vacant home with absent drama, the semblance of activity.

'Right, time for dinner,' she eventually says. He doesn't

hear. The volume is still turned up and his ears are partially covered.

It isn't until nine o'clock, when their Hindi soaps finish, that she goes to the kitchen and makes fresh chapattis to go with the vegetable she made in the afternoon. She cooked mashed aubergines and onions with turmeric and tangy mango powder until they were soft and gooey. She puts a small dish of it in the microwave, pushes the door shut, and feels for the textured stickers that allow her to find the buttons with her fingertips — a circle, a triangle and a little car-shaped bubble.

While it warms up, she unwraps the dough she made earlier from its sticky cling-film cover, carefully kneads it with her hands and rolls small balls out of it like a time-old ritual. She dips each one into a Tupperware box of flour and rolls it into thin, flat discs with her rolling pin. She can barely see, since retinal deterioration has eliminated most of her sight, but she chooses not to be helped.

She serves him as she always has — he hasn't cooked a morsel in decades and she prefers it that way. They eat silently at the Formica kitchen table, sitting on wheelie chairs so they can whizz about to get the salt or a cup of water, wrapping mouthfuls of bhaji with ripped-up chapatti and scooping it into their mouths. He no longer tolerates spicy food and eats his food with gherkins and onions in sweet vinegar, while she nibbles on a green chilli.

'The phone's ringing,' says Padma.

She washes up while he goes to the study and answers. It's

Sachin. Laxman holds the receiver with one hand while steadying himself with the other to sit at a small pine bureau. They've had it ever since they bought it for their children to revise for their exams — it's on its last legs but they don't throw anything out unless it's beyond saving. Sachin suggested they bought a new one when the hinges went but Laxman replaced them. Then, when the knobs on the draws began to loosen, he tightened the screws up with a spanner. He even sanded it down and re-varnished it a few times over the years. It has the veneer of youth, like his body, a patched-up canvas saved from the scrapheap by his surgeon's toolkit. If the bureau was strong enough to hold the weight of his heavy laptop, it was worth saving.

He flips open the lid of the machine slowly and within seconds it zips with life.

'I've been wanting to talk to you,' says Laxman. 'The damn thing, it still won't print.'

'Try clicking some more of the icons,' Sachin says. 'It's different with the new operating system.'

Laxman moves the mouse around and clicks a button with the icon of a disk. Nothing happens. Another looks like a paintbrush. Nothing happens again. A few buttons make the cursor move to the centre, and then to the right side of the screen, where it flashes at him like a pesky fly his swat has missed. He knows he doesn't want a text box or picture so he knows to skip those buttons over; he has used this machine for years. He learnt to use a computer by himself when he was seventy-five. He read the manuals line by line, making notes and memorising them with diligence. He isn't going to give up yet.

'Will it still not print?' asks Sachin.

The screen of buttons seems to him a secret code that he can't crack. Less of them make sense each time the computer updates itself.

'Do you want to come over on Saturday? Then you can fix it,' Laxman says.

'We can't Saturday, Dad. We're having friends over. How about rebooting?'

It's either his plans and paperwork or job — and then there are these *friends*. Laxman regrets the invitation, twirls the cord at the end of the receiver. He dreads the day when the whole world will look as scrambled as this screen, evolved beyond his comprehension. Then he fears he will be dependent on them.

'Always busy,' he says, moving his index finger furiously around the mouse pad. But before there is a chance for discussion, Padma walks in.

'Enough *ghit mit*,' she says, raising one hand and slicing it through the air like a karate chop. 'Sachin has things to do.' Her intuition has compensated for her eyes, and neither of them has ever wanted to be imposing. Laxman ends the call abruptly. His wife's glare reminds him of his ability to rub people up the wrong way.

They get changed and climb into a high bed with a hard mattress, like the ones they had in Bombay, draped with white, veil-like netting. Laxman looks at a black-and-white photograph of them on his bedside. They both have jet black hair and smooth skin. He is wearing a suit and she is in a salwar kameez not very different to the ones she wears now. It was taken when the idea of him becoming a doctor in England was barely realisable. He had never even been further than Delhi and would go hungry during medical school to save money. He would sleep with the guilt that his mother's jewellery had been sold for his schooling. Each night that photo reminded him to be thankful that his family would never want for anything again.

'Hari Om. Hari Om. Hari Om.'

§

The next day, Padma unfolds her cane, wears her soft walking shoes and socks, and goes outside, while Laxman talks on the phone to the bank manager who, out of kindness, makes the time. They live on a quiet road off a long high street that ends at the station. She can make out the shadows of cars but stays on the same side of the road to be safe. That way, she only has to cross two quiet roads. It is a walk she has been doing ever since they moved here, though the distance has reduced considerably. She used to walk all the way to the Heath, stroll around until she felt as though she had left the city. Now, it is too tiring – her knees hurt and can only be stretched for so long – but being able to roam freely is enough.

Sometimes, like today, she grows short of breath and has to stop at a bench halfway down. She sits, rests her cane on her knee and closes her eyes. It is milder than it has been. The cold never has suited her and she remembers the breeze the first winter she ever spent in England, when she couldn't believe you could live where the air hurt your face. She has grown accustomed to that, but other things still feel foreign. She thinks about what her sons are doing. They must be at work. And her grandchildren. They must be busy with their studies. She was raised in a bustling house of grandparents, aunts, cousins, neighbours. She wonders why her own family don't stay nearby; why people here choose to live in bubbles of seclusion. She pulls out a mobile phone from her pocket that Sachin gave her for emergencies. She only ever receives calls on it, as the tiny numbers on the buttons are invisible to her, and she has never learnt to use it. She hears a pair of block heels hitting the pavement and a woman who smells of lavender takes the place next to her.

'It's a lovely day, isn't it? Lovely day.'

Padma looks at her. 'Lov-ely,' she says. She rarely speaks English so her 'v' comes out like a round 'w'.

'Do you have grandchildren?' the woman asks. Padma looks at her to check she is being addressed. She can make out the contours of black wavy hair and breasts.

'Two,' she says. 'One son in London. Another in America.'

'Well, at least you have one close by,' she says, putting an arm around Padma's shoulders. Her clasp is warm and swallows up her small frame like stuffing.

'Yes,' says Padma, wondering if she has misunderstood the woman's optimism.

The woman shuffles up the bench, removes something from her handbag and seems to be applying it to her face; make-up perhaps. Padma wonders what colour it might be, remembering the brown lipstick she once wore in the days when they went to dinner parties and weddings, before their friends became housebound or moved on. Soon, she hears the heavy whirr of a bus pulling up and the woman is gone.

On her way back home, Padma starts feeling short of breath again. She struggles to make the air pass from her mouth down to her stomach, as though there isn't enough space. There is no other bench to stop at so she presses on: she has never spent a day in bed, not even with the flu. Her chest begins to tighten like there's a clenched fist around her heart, but she is almost there. She pushes on, one step after the next, using her cane not as a substitute for sight but as a third leg. By the time she approaches the door to her building, the pain wrenches inside her, and she collapses into a heap against the frame.

'Are you alright?' She can make out a tall man in a skullcap and black suit with a low voice. She tries to breathe but it feels like her chest has been stapled together and fastened tight. An ambulance is called. Laxman is summoned from upstairs – he is still on the phone but somehow hears the man at the door – and soon they are speeding down the high street with flashing lights and sirens.

§

The pain subsides and Padma lies in a ward, fatigued, next to a woman whose daughter speaks to her though she barely responds, and opposite another woman who is bedbound with an oxygen mask and alone. She has stabilised, the doctors say, and she has to rest. Beside her, Laxman, who has spent the night there, awakes from a long nap in his coat and deerstalker hat. Two women come over and hover at the end of her bed. She can't make out what they are saying, though they seem concerned. One gives her some pink and white tablets, which she swallows with water.

'Lovely,' she says, beaming over Padma with a smile.

A trolley is brought through the ward and stops next to her. A man gives her a plate and begins to remove the plastic covering. She looks at it expecting her worst nightmare: steak.

'Asian vegetarian,' he says. 'Is that right?'

She makes out a plate of rice, daal and a stew of vegetables. She nods with relief. The man wishes her a good afternoon and moves on to serve the woman opposite. She finishes it quickly, ravenous, before lying back to chant the Hanuman Chalisa, a six-minute prayer she silently recites every day, which today she will chant eleven times. She shuts her eyes and begins to sing the words to herself. She doesn't move or pause, not even to answer the phone when it vibrates loudly against the wood of the bedside cabinet. It must be Sachin; he's the only one who normally calls. She is absorbed in the comforting monotony of the chant. The only certainty has become its hypnotic rhythm. Besides, she doesn't want to tell him what has happened.

When Laxman awakes, he removes his hat and sees she is deep in concentration. He knows not to disturb her and instead thinks about their children. He considers whether to tell them their mother is unwell, until she turns to her side and it is apparent she has finished chanting. By the time she does so she knows what he is thinking, and he knows she has cottoned on.

'Don't tell them, Laxman,' she says. 'Please don't.'

He looks at her with bloodshot eyes. He doesn't normally want to worry them, either. They are busy enough. But this is different; she has never been in hospital before. He knows Sachin will be furious if he doesn't learn of this. He removes his thick, bifocal spectacles and wipes them with his bobbly M&S jumper. She turns into a haze of blurry green and white, the shades of her long gown.

'In any case, I'm fine,' she insists. 'Let's ask them to get you some lunch.'

'You're not fine,' he says, but when he puts his glasses back on he thinks she may be right. The pink seems to have returned to her cheeks and the few lines on her forehead appear to him smaller than ever. She pulls herself off the bed and there, standing beside him, she looks strong.

Without giving him a chance to settle the matter, she gets off the bed unaided and goes to the ladies. He remembers that it is the middle of the week and Sachin will be at work. When he comes home he will have to help Rhea with her homework. Before he has a chance to decide what to do,

Padma returns with a cuppa-soup and two slices of toast magiced out of no-where.

'Here you are,' she says, clearing the small wheelie table of her things and laying the table for him as though they are at home.

'Perhaps you are right,' he says. 'They don't need to be bothered.'

He sits there and slurps the soup, swallowing the soggy lumps of toast he has dunked into it like croutons. She begins chanting once again, this time a different prayer — one in her regional tongue that her mother taught her and she taught her children. She chants desperately as if to connect with them. She chants until she is lulled into a deep, long sleep.

Laxman has learnt from one of the doctors that the hospital is having a public meeting that day. As a retired doctor, he thinks he might have something worthwhile to say. He reads a circular on the cork board in the corridor while Padma sleeps. It will be in the auditorium on the ground floor at three, it says, and visitors will have the chance to ask questions. He wants to tell them waiting times need to be improved — he had to wait months for a scan when his stomach refused to digest anything and the kilos fell off him. He wants to tell them his GP referred him to a string of specialists when they should have just admitted him for a day. Not that his GP cared about his wellbeing — in his day you treated your patients like people, not bodies.

There is time; the meeting doesn't begin for another hour.

His body aches from sleeping vertically on the armchair by Padma's side and he knows another night there will leave him as stiff as his thick computer manual. A pinch in his lower back forces him to sit down. As he begins to write down his questions for the meeting on a scrap of paper, he sees Padma's phone vibrate on the bedside cabinet. It is Sachin. He considers ignoring it, but it rumbles loudly against the wood and he doesn't know how to make it stop.

'You don't have to worry,' he says. 'Mum has just had a small heart attack... No, no, don't worry, she is okay.' He tries to soften the blow, but when he says it out loud, it feels like a small balloon has just burst inside his round stomach. 'No, there's no need to come. After work? Oh.'

He looks at his gold watch. He has a few hours before Sachin will turn up, so he decides to go down to the meeting, while Padma's eyes are still peacefully shut, her mouth slightly ajar as it always is when she sleeps. If things go well, they should be able to go home soon, he thinks. He sits down and completes his list of questions, then carefully drapes a green cellular blanket over her and goes downstairs. He still has it in him to make the hospital a better place, he thinks. He might be old but he has known medicine in Britain for over sixty years, ever since he arrived by boat on a rainy September morning at Southampton dock, with little more than the kurta on his back.

§

After the meeting, he takes the lift straight back up to the ward, to make sure he arrives in time to tell Padma their son is coming. He stops at the door to the ward to use the gel in the dispenser; rubs it into the leathery creases of his skin. He will tell her how pleased he is that they accepted his questions. They only had time to listen to a few, but everyone else was allowed to put a paper in a special box, including him. He is sure that the committee will take his points on board and things will change. When they consider his ideas, waiting times and service will improve, he thinks. He will tell her all of this when he gets back.

For a moment, he is still a doctor in a ward like this one, wearing his shirtsleeves rolled up, his tie tucked in, a long white coat and a stethoscope around his neck. His children used to play doctors and nurses with that stethoscope at home. For them, playing doctors and nurses was just a game: the thought of anyone being a patient with anything more than a scratch was barely possible. It isn't until he sees an energetic man in a grey suit pacing up and down the corridor that he is brought back to the present.

'It's a good thing you told me, Dad.'

'You weren't supposed to be here yet,' he says, frantic. 'She didn't want you to be bothered.'

But from Sachin's face he knows it is too late. The curtain around Padma's bed is drawn and, through a crack, he sees a group of doctors in their smocks crowded around her, resuscitating her small body. He looks away and sits down in the ward. They wait for what seems like hours but it is over quickly. He hears the familiar constant beep of the flat line and he knows it has happened. He wants his hat; to wrap it around his head and cover his ears to suffocate his hearing.

§

'Let's pack your things,' says Sachin.

Laxman watches as his son takes a suitcase from a cupboard in the hallway and begins to remove shirts and trousers from the hangers, folding them into piles that seem to sum up what little is left worth continuing for. Laxman doesn't speak until his son opens Padma's wardrobe, realises what it contains, and closes it again.

'You don't want me moving in,' he says, as an order rather than a question.

He can just about hold his own with the internet, but he has seen his parents and his brothers grow old — he knows what is in store. Sachin holds up a moth-eaten bathrobe and looks at it sheepishly.

'I think it's time to throw this out,' he says.

Laxman is silent. He knows he will soon be a decrepit old rag, and then they'll want to throw him out too. The robe seems fine to him, and has served him well for over a decade. It holds his past in its mangled fleece. Why is everyone so drawn to the 'new'? He looks around him, at the mirror they were given by the woman next door, the curtains Padma stitched with her own hands, the carpets they had fitted once their children left home. Everything around him stands for something else. He sees no reason to throw it out.

'I don't want to move in anyway. I'll be just fine alone,' he says.

Sachin continues to the dresser, takes the picture in a frame and places it in a suitcase between two shirts. Laxman watches him open the drawers and take out his underwear and odd woollen socks, some fraying jumpers, all of them clean and freshly-ironed: his wife's legacy. Sachin holds up a fine cashmere cardigan that he gave his father one Christmas, with the labels still on. Laxman was saving it for a special day.

'Right, I think we are nearly there.'

Laxman watches his son from the edge of the bed. His back still hurts and he just wants to sit. He wants to spend the rest of the day staring at the computer screen and finding out what the buttons do — it is his version of chanting. But he waits patiently as his son packs up his things and takes the suitcases downstairs. Sachin returns after depositing the last bag in the boot of the car, and there is nothing left to do.

'You can't stay here,' he says. He rests a calming hand on Laxman's shoulder, to encourage him to come, but Laxman doesn't flinch. 'Besides,' he continues. 'We want you to come.'

Laxman pushes himself off the bed onto his feet and goes over to the window. Outside, the sun is setting over brown brick buildings. In the distance, the arch of Wembley stadium juts out of the skyline like a white rainbow. He remembers when it was first built and he didn't like the way it disturbed the view he had always known, but he has grown accustomed to it, and now it feels like it has always been there.

'Why don't we take your gherkins? And onions?' says Sachin.

Afterwards, they drive through North London until they reach a red-brick terrace with large bay windows that Laxman remembers visiting. It is a pretty house with begonias growing in the flower boxes hung along the railings outside. The door opens and his daughter-in-law helps Sachin with the bags. Laxman lifts himself out of the car with his arms and holds his tense back as he straightens up. He decides he'll go straight upstairs and check the hardness of the spare bed. He removes his furry hat, hangs it on the banister, and looks at his watch.

'Do you think we can get Hindi TV here?' he asks, before his two grandchildren in their pyjamas run to him, insist on him coming up to see their room and their toys, and somehow, a first in as long as his memory serves him, time runs away with itself.

Author Biographies

Mahsuda Snaith is a Leicester based writer of short stories, novels and plays. She is the winner of the *SI Leeds Literary Prize 2014, Bristol Short Story Prize 2014* and was a finalist in the *Mslexia Novel Competition 2013*. As well as working as a supply teacher, Mahsuda leads creative writing workshops. She has performed her work at literary festivals, recently finished writing a play and really enjoys rowing, though only at home on a machine where no one can see her. To find out more visit www.mahsudasnaith.com.

Deepa Anappara is a graduate of the City University's Certificate in Novel Writing course (now known as the Novel Studio). Her short stories have won third prize in the Asham award, second prize in the Bristol Short Story Prize and first prize in the Asian Writer Short Story contest. These stories appear in *Once Upon a Time There Was a Traveller* (Virago), *Bristol Short Story Prize Anthology Vol 6* (Bristol Review of Books) and *Five Degrees* (Dahlia Publishing).

Farhana Shaikh is a writer and publisher born in Leicester. She is the founding editor of *The Asian Writer*, an online magazine championing Asian literature. She manages Dahlia Publishing, a small press keen to publish regional and diverse writing. She has facilitated creative writing workshops and judged writing competitions in the UK and India. Farhana lives in Leicester with her husband and their two children. She hosts Writers Meet Up Leicester and tweets about books and publishing @farhanashaikh

Farrah Yusuf was born in Pakistan and grew up in London. A graduate of LSE and UCL, she is a solicitor turned charity worker who began writing fiction two years ago. Her first short story, *Milk*, was published in 'Five Degrees: The Asian Writer Short Story Prize 2012 Anthology'. Her short stories, *Burnt* and *Zoya* were published in the SADAA 'Against the Grain' 2013 collection and *Caged* is a finalist in the Writeidea 2014 Prize Short Story Competition. She took part in Kali Theatre TalkBack 2014 to develop her first play and is currently working on a novel. www.farrahyusuf.com

Jocelyn Watson The Asian Women's Writers Collective was Jocelyn Watson's first writing home. She has a mixed racial background; her mother is Indian and her father English. In 2011 she gave up full time employment as a human rights lawyer to focus full time on her writing and has subsequently won various prizes including The Freedom from Torture Short Story Competition for *London Plane*. She is one of the Alumni of the Arts Council funded Cultural Leadership Programme and in 2011 was sponsored to attend the Jaipur Literature Festival. In 2013 she was the winner of the UK Asian Writer Short Story Competition for

The Gardener. She is active in feminist, BME and socialist politics.

Amna Khokher has a BA in English Literature and Creative Writing from the University of Warwick and an MA in Creative Writing from Bath Spa University. Her fiction has been shortlisted and longlisted for a number of competitions including The Asian Writer Short Story Competition 2012 and 2013 and the Fish Short Story Prize 2013 and has appeared in women's literary magazine Mslexia. She has performed her work at literary festivals and is writing her first novel.

Reetinder Boparai was born in India, but grew up in Britain and has lived here for over 40 years. She has a BSc. Hons. in Pharmacology from King's College London and a MSc. in Social Science Research Methods from Middlesex University. Reetinder is a researcher having worked in local government and in academia. She enjoys writing creatively and over the years has spent time crafting her words into short stories and poems. She is currently writing her first novel. Her story 'Deception' was published in *Five Degrees: The Asian Writer Short Story Prize 2012 anthology*.
She lives in Reading with her husband and son.

Nilopar Uddin is a writer based in London. Nilopar's writing has been published in *Five Degrees: The Asian Writer Short Story Prize 2012* anthology, the Huffington

Post, and pygmygiant.com. She is also a dual qualified lawyer, who has practised in England and Wales and in New York, and has contributed to legal texts including the book Good Governance and Resource Management in Africa. Nilopar is currently studying on City University's MA in Creative Writing and lives with her husband and two daughters who provides with ample inspiration for her writing.

Rosie Dastgir is the author of the novel, *A Small Fortune*, (Penguin US, Quercus UK) . Her writing has been published in the *New York Times Magazine, Stella Magazine*, and the *Prospect blog*. She is a contributing writer for www.spitalfieldslife.com, where she teaches weekend creative writing classes. Her stage play, *Bevan's Baby*, featured as part of the Arcola Theatre's PlayWrought New Writing Festival in London. She wrote and presented *The Art of Home*, a documentary for BBC Radio 4, about the importance of roots for writers and artists. Her first radio play was broadcast last year on BBC Radio 3.

Huma Qureshi is an author and freelance journalist. Her first book, *In Spite of Oceans: Migrant Voices*, a collection of stories of south Asian family life, was published in October 2014 by The History Press. *In Spite of Oceans* won the John C Laurence Award from The Authors' Foundation for promoting understanding between cultures. Huma's short stories have been published in Mslexia and Psychologies. In

2014, she placed second in the national Ink Tears Short Story Competition. She is now working on a novel.

Susmita Bhattacharya is from Mumbai, India. She sailed around the world in oil tankers with her husband before dropping anchor in Wales, where she received an M.A. in Creative Writing from Cardiff University in 2006. Several of her short stories and poems have been published in the UK and internationally, including journals and magazines such as Wasafiri, Planet- the Welsh Internationalist, Litro, Eleven Eleven (USA), The View from Here, Riptide, Commuterlit.com, the BBC and anthologies Rarebit- New Welsh Writing, Stories for Homes, Far Flung and Foreign. She lives in Plymouth with her husband, two daughters and the neighbour's cat. She facilitates creative writing in the community and blogs at http://susmita-bhattacharya.blogspot.co.uk. Her debut novel, The Normal State of Mind, Parthian UK, will be out in January 2015. Connect on Twitter @Susmitatweets

Palo Stickland was born in the Indian Punjab and brought up in Glasgow where she worked as a teacher. From studies in creative writing at Strathclyde University and the Open University she has gained two post-graduate qualifications in creative writing. Success in publication has been in anthologies in Scotland and in winning the Asian Writer Poetry Competition twice. Her novel *Finding Takri* was published in August 2013. She is working on her second novel.

Priya Khanchandani Priya's essays and journalism about the arts and culture can be found in Wasafiri, Disegno Magazine, Conde Nast Traveller and India's Sunday Guardian. She recently contributed to Bloomsbury's forthcoming Encyclopedia of Design. Her story, *A Done Deal*, won her a nomination for the Asian Writer Short Story Prize 2012. Priya is a graduate of the Royal College of Art's MA in the History of Design where she received the Dissertation Prize for her research about contemporary Indian cities, and has an undergraduate degree from Cambridge University. She curates contemporary design and art and works as a Development Manager at the Victoria and Albert Museum, where she is responsible for strategising and maximising funding for the acquisition of new objects. Before pursuing her creative interests full-time, Priya was a lawyer at a magic circle law firm.

Discover new and diverse voices in literature
www.theasianwriter.co.uk

More titles from Dahlia Publishing
www.dahliapublishing.co.uk

Happy Birthday to Me: A collection of Contemporary Asian Writing, 2010, £8.99

Bombay Baby, Leela Soma, 2011, £12.99

Five Degrees: The Asian Writer Short Story Prize 2012, 2012, £8.99

Finding Takri, Palo Stickland, 2013, £12.99

Tiger, Tiger (ebook), Anjana Basu, 2014, £1.95

Forthcoming

This Green and Pleasant Land, Ruth Ahmed, 2015

Moroccan Tales of Love and Disaster, Kirstin Ruth Bratt, 2015